GRANNY'S BASKETS

from the Secret Valley of Singing Crystals

Carol C. McFall

Order this book online at www.trafford.com
or email orders@trafford.com

Most Trafford titles are also available at major online book retailers.

Printed in Victoria, BC, Canada.

ISBN: 978-1-4269-2320-3 (sc)
ISBN: 978-1-4269-2321-0 (hc)

Library of Congress Control Number: 2009912364

*Our mission is to efficiently provide the world's finest, most comprehensive book publishing
service, enabling every author to experience success. To find out how to publish your book, your
way, and have it available worldwide, visit us online at www.trafford.com*

Trafford rev. 3/12/10

www.trafford.com

North America & international
toll-free: 1 888 232 4444 (USA & Canada)
phone: 250 383 6864 ♦ fax: 812 355 4082

Thanks to everything and everyone, to planet earth and its beings, to friends and relatives who were and still are a part of the journey to publish my first book, GRANNY'S BASKETS.

I don't know when it will be published but GRANNY'S WHAT NOTS is in the works—a collection of mini tall tales — A COOL MONSTER, BUNGLING BUNNY, THE BLACK PEARL, RADDLEHEAD ROBIN and many other bedtime stories .

Special thanks to my husband, Dick, for his encouraging words; to son, Rick, for his patience and instructions about how to use my computer word processor ; to son, Tim, for loving memories of his lifetime with us.

Contents

Mysterious Disappearances

At the west gate, one of the armor-suited guards astride a royal white steed, shifted his lance into the ready position and waited. Something, someone was crossing the desert, rapidly approaching Castletown. In her tower bedroom a princess wakened to morning bustle in the castle and to whinnies in the stables. She glanced out her window and noticed the dust. *Not enough for a caravan. The guards have put up their lances.*

The princess dressed hurriedly and then tip-toed down a stone staircase. The west gate was already creaking open. *He brings his horses.* She glanced over her shoulder and scooted out a back door. *He knows.*

Boldly she stepped in front of his horses and shouted at him, "Where do you get your horses?"

A bemused, smiling horse seller shook his finger at her.

"You might be hurt doing that one day."

Her hands went to her hips and she planted her feet.

"Where?"

His grin widened.

"In a magical place. Not a place of just black and white horses, a place of wild horses, horses of many different colors, in a valley beyond the mountains."

Suddenly he was beside her. She was looking up into his eyes.

"Father says we must stay behind our walls where we are safe from rogues and marauders who might harm us or steal what we have. No one from Castletown ventures into the desert."

He shook his head.

"Hidden treasures may be found if a person dares to cross deserts; if a person dares to climb mountains; if a person knows what to look for."

He made a sweeping gesture with his hand.

"Imagine a sleepy wide river, a roaring spectacular waterfall, a green valley beyond this dusty desert. That is where I come from."

He could see that the princess was fascinated. He smiled at her. There was a momentary silence between them.

Ever so quickly, his expression changed and his voice was almost stern.

"Crossing deserts can be dangerous. Many unwary have been drowned in the plains of your desert. Mysterious raging rivers appear and disappear, carve canyons and leave dry washes. I bring horses to Castletown, only a few times a year, in a dry season, I call my selling-horse moons."

He watched her eyes widen. She was frowning.

"Do your mother and father live there, beyond the mountains?"

He shook his head.

"No, but I am not alone in the valley. There are others, like the wizard who can soar like an eagle."

There was a twinkle in the horse seller's eyes as he spoke about the wizard. The princess seemed to be drawn into the very depths of his hazel eyes.

I wonder how old he is? Muscular arms—eyes compelling, fascinating, ancient. Why do I think his eyes are ancient? Why, why am I remembering grandmother's saying—Some are wiser than their years?

She was fascinated by his calm deep voice and she wanted to hear more. He was patting his horse's neck, leaning forward to speak to her.

"I find beautiful, strange flowers in my valley at times in places I call life-markers. Blossoms open sometimes in the darkest of nights. Flowers so fragrant they evoke music, part of a whole song the valley knows how to sing. Crystals of the mountain, with the slightest encouragement, sing their own notes too."

She turned her head to one side; gazed up at the clouds; stood there staring, longing to be in a different place, to be a part of his entrancing story.

How can I get to the valley of horses? Guards at all four gates. Mother, father will not allow it. No one except the seller of horses leaves Castletown.

The princess tried to imagine Castletown without walls, without armored guards.

He crosses the desert. Why can't I? Grandmother said our wall building began a long time ago. She said she knew a secret. I remember her story.

It was a time of discontent and explosive angers. A strange merchant visited and presented us with the gift of Ynnaline, just before a plague struck Castletown. Ynnaline saved us from disaster. Most of the precious liquid was used up combating the plague. The few drops left in the original bottle were transferred to a smaller bottle and kept in a storage room behind the throne.

One day she heard a tap, tap, tapping behind the throne. She opened the door to the storage room and a black bird flew out. It was carrying a little bottle in its claw and she thought she heard it say, "Nevermore, Nevermore," as it flew away. She said she couldn't tell anyone. Who would believe her?

When next the doctor came to retrieve the bottle, to treat an illness, he reported the bottle missing. The castle was searched, but of course, it was never found.

The princess was sighing, staring into space.

It's not fair. Hardly anyone even remembers it happened. It wasn't desert marauders and yet Castletown is still building heavier, higher walls. We don't venture into the desert and we don't climb mountains.

The seller of horses looked over his shoulder at the guards at the west gate and then glanced back at the princess.

She is ignoring me.

He straightened up in his saddle and tightened the reins. She glanced at the west gate.

Is it possible—drowning in our desert? Is there a green valley of horses? The music a horse seller hears. Could I hear it? Could I ride a horse of a different color? Oh, no! He's preparing to leave.

One guard was watching them.

The princess leaned against the horse seller's horse and whispered to the fascinating young man, "Take me to the flowers, the crystals and the many colored horses."

He shook his head; spoke slowly and softly.

"It is a very dangerous journey, even for me. And wanting is not enough. You know that no one enters or leaves this fortress. Castletown guards only allow me through the gates because your father wants more and more and more black horses and white horses for his ever bigger, ever more spectacular royal tournaments."

She shook long blonde hair out of her face.

It sounds like criticism. How dare he?

She almost shouted, "Jousts need black horses, white horses— winners, losers—There must be a visible difference. The king has decreed and everyone agreed. We must know our champion at a glance, by what color horse he rides."

The horse seller's mount, the dappled black and white horse he rode was kicking up dust—almost prancing in place. The princess looked down at the prancing hoofs and looked down at her own feet collecting dust. She stood silent for a few moments, and then kicked up some dust of her own wondering.

Why am I attracted to this stranger? Could it be because I remember grandmother's stories of a visitor from a strange land, the stranger who brought her the gift of Ynnaline before there were walls around Castletown?

She looked up at the horse seller. The reins in his hand were against the neck of his horse. It was turning. He was about to ride away.

"I almost believe you about the horses, about the valley but you have to show them to me."

The horse seller was about to say *No*, again when he looked into beautiful eyes—soft, almost blue, curious wide eyes.

Innocent, trusting eyes—I could lose myself in them.

It took some determination and more than one deep breath. Finally he found his voice again. He leaned toward her and whispered.

"Perhaps, one day we might fool the guards."

She raised her voice.

"Don't go. How did you find the valley of horses?"

The horse seller loosened the reins again. He sat back in his saddle and looked far away and up to the left.

"It was a long time ago. My grandmother told me a story."

The horse seller's eyes dropped down a little. He was still looking off to the left. It was as if he were remembering, hearing his grandmother's voice. When he spoke again, he looked a princess in the eye and told her that his grandmother had been a prisoner in a dungeon of her own father's castle.

And that one dark night when she was lonely and despondent she heard a cricket singing. She began to breathe in rhythm with the cricket's song. The cricket sang about a raging river, magnificent mountains, the daunting desert and a lost valley of horses.

He said that at first his grandmother was sure she knew what she heard. But then, after a few days had gone by she began to wonder if she might have only dreamed that a cricket sang to her. Still she encouraged him.

"If there is a valley of horses, you'll find it one day."

The horse seller's horse was restless, twitching its ears and throwing its head. The princess stroked its nose.

"I want to find it too. I know I can do it."

The horse seller reached out, almost touching her cheek.

"Perhaps you could. Together we might. What a bit of luck this is— I don't enter through the same gate each time I come to Castletown. I use all four gates to the castle and so all the guards know me."

"That can't be lucky," said the princess.

He shook his head, gestured with both hands as if he were gathering air into a huge ball.

"Yes, yes, it is lucky because they don't expect me to come and go through one gate, alone. They all let me pass through with my trusty black and white steed. They all know my horse too."

She stamped her foot.

"How can that be lucky?"

He whispered.

"*When you wear the garment you will know. Next time I come to the castle, you must have fashioned a horse seller's suit, clothes to wear, just like mine. I will bring some paint with me when I come.*"

She looked around. The guards were distracted by a dust devil swirling not far from the gate. The princess kissed a horse seller on the cheek. But then she huffed at him.

"I don't understand, but I'll think about it."

She was running away from him and away from the guards. She thought she heard him whisper, "*Until we meet again.*"

What if someone saw me kiss him? How could I kiss a horse seller? Can I learn to sew? Should I? Should I ride a horse of a different color?

He was riding to the stables. When she reached the main entrance to the castle, she was almost breathless. Suddenly the stone staircase was disheartening. Her whole body felt heavy and her feet were dragging. She didn't know if she could climb the steps.

One step—*I don't know how clothes are put together.*

Step two—*My clothes have always been chosen for me.*

Step three—*I wear what is already laid out for me.*

Step four—*It is always what I have done.*

She sat down for a few moments to catch her breath.

There is no way.

The back of her hand went to her forehead.

I can't do it by myself.

She collapsed. Her head was resting on the back of hands crossed at the wrist and clutching her knees.

She imagined she heard the horse seller say, "*You can do it. Yes, YES!* "

She straightened up—reached out as if his hand were there, as if he were pulling her to her feet. She looked up at the rest of the steps and took some deep breaths.

Someone knows how to sew! I will find a way to ride a horse of a different color.

She almost ran the rest of the way up the steps.

She saw him from her tower room window—erect, poised young man, riding a dappled black and white horse through the south gate of Castletown. Her heart fluttered and she began to long to see him again, even before he disappeared from her sight—circling, circling to the right and finally out of sight—far away on the horizon.

What is happening to me? What am I feeling?

She began to ask the king and queen more and more questions and one question was very disturbing— so disturbing the king and queen didn't answer her, just shook their heads and looked at one another.

"Are we prisoners in our own Castletown?" brought no reply from the king and queen.

After a restless night of dreaming about the horse seller and the valley of horses, the princess shouted at the king and queen.

"Where do my clothes come from?"

The king lifted an eyebrow and looked over at the queen. She spoke quietly to her royal daughter.

"There is a dressmaker who makes clothes for everyone in Castletown."

The princess calmed down, cleared her throat and spoke in her normal tone of voice.

"What is her name and where does she make the clothes? It is time for me to meet the dressmaker and to choose new clothes for myself."

The king and queen whispered to one another.

The king said, "Some young princesses go through rebellious stages when they have to find things out for themselves. It's nothing to worry about. Let her go to the dressmaker. Let her order her own clothes. What harm can there be in it? Nothing to worry about—"

There was an amused sparkle in the queen's eye and the corners of her mouth turned up. She winked at the king and gave the princess directions to the shop of the dressmaker.

"Go, order a new dress. Melinda's designs are pleasing. She fills our royal orders. A princess can always use another new dress."

The princess was almost skipping to the stable. She mounted a white royal steed and rode to the dressmaker's shop.

It might take a little daring but it is not impossible.

The dressmaker was very surprised to see a princess at her humble shop. She bowed and curtsied.

"What is your wish?"

"A suit, just like the horse sellers, and it must be ready in seven days," the princess demanded in as stern a royal tone as she could muster.

The dressmaker hesitated. There was a frown on her face.

If the king and queen see their princess in anything but royal clothes, my reputation will be ruined. I can't refuse a royal request. What can I do? What can I do?

Her voice was quivering and her hands were shaking when finally she said, "You shall have it."

The princess left the dressmaker's shop with a light heart and a spring in her step.

Next moon on the 8th day, he'll return to the castle to fetch me.

Melinda sat down to think about what she should do. She was leaning on the cutting table, elbow bent, head in her hand, when a bolt of fine silk material caught her eye.

Royal dressmakers aren't easily discouraged and Melinda was a resourceful person. In a few moments she gathered her thoughts and her tools together.

I can create a royal horse seller's suit.

Cutting into a fine silk brocade, adding jeweled beads, she began her sewing, not knowing how or what she was about to create. Once the work was begun, the suit almost created itself, and it was spectacular—a work of art. Melinda stared at her creation.

The king and queen may not like it, but it is a royal suit AND acceptable. My reputation is saved.

She delivered the new creation to the castle on the seventh day, as promised.

When the princess saw her new suit, she couldn't wait to put it on and parade around the throne room. The king looked twice, to see if it really was the princess. The queen looked away from her daughter and almost stared into the eyes of the king, as if asking him what they should do.

Neither one spoke a word about her new clothes, her new look.

They see my new suit. They could say something. Why do they pretend they are too busy to comment? Why are they ignoring me? No response at all— it doesn't matter. He comes tomorrow.

She turned her back on the king and queen, exited the throne room and returned to her bedroom to change her clothes.

The king leaned over to the queen and whispered.

"It was difficult not to laugh, not to say a word–watching her prance around in that outrageous outfit."

On the eighth day, the handsome young horse seller returned to the castle and sold his horses. As he was leaving the stables, the princess ran to greet him in her new suit. He leaned down to her and whispered in her ear.

"Did you sew a suit like mine?"

"I'm wearing the suit," she shouted gleefully.

The young man just shook his head.

"Look, look at my suit and look again at yours. We both wear pants now! Just not the same kind."

The princess wrinkled her brows, stamped her foot and gritted her teeth.

He is not recognizing how clever I have been to get a horse seller's suit to wear.

She was stomping back to the castle but before she reached the front entrance, she turned to look at the young man again. Her heart began to flutter and she fainted.

When the princess opened her eyes, he was leaning over her, almost face to face –a tender caring expression in his eyes.

A strange new fragrance in the air awakened some kind of music, a haunting and almost melancholy melody inside her.

What's this in my hand? A—a—flower—?

9

Before she could say anything he mounted his horse and rode away through the north gate of Castletown.

The princess brushed dust from her new suit. She took the flower to her tower room and sat on her bed.

His eyes, the fragrance of this flower, the music inside me.

Part of a song, an unfinished song called to her. She was longing to hear the whole song. The more she longed, the more questions she asked her mother and father.

"Where does the seller of horses comes from?"

"We don't need to know, as long as he keeps bringing us black and white horses," said the king.

"How do you know he will keep bringing us horses?"

"He always comes this time of year, two or three times, after a new moon."

The queen patted her daughter on the shoulder.

"Now go along with you. Be the good princess you have always been. And don't ask so many questions."

She leaned over and spoke in whispers to the king.

"I am wondering if the horse seller might pose some kind of danger to our princess."

There was a concerned scowl on the king's face.

"Although, Castletown is secure and defended, I'm giving the guards orders to watch her very carefully when the horse seller is inside our walls."

Singing Crystals

In a cave near the top of a mountain, another rare delicate flower was unfolding its petals. He bent over to look at it. His pants pocket caught on a protruding crystal and set the crystal singing.

Its vibrations and overtones were loosening it from its niche in the side of the cave. He turned around just in time to catch it in his hand. It was still singing its haunting note—a note that filled him with longing. A tear trickled down his cheek.

She is so beautiful.

Far below, beside a flowing river, stones in a semi-circular ring of stones, began to sing their part of the valley song, as if in answer to the crystal's longing note. Horses began to gather at the stones. The horse seller was watching them.

Fewer black horses, fewer white horses—their numbers decreasing. I cannot, must not, continue to sell blacks; must not sell whites.

No one in Castletown, except the princess, noticed the handsome horse seller hadn't come on the eighth day. She watched for him from her tower window and she paced back and forth. Finally she went to the stables and mounted a horse.

She rode around to all four gates asking, "Have you seen the horse seller? Have you seen the horse seller?"

Four no's—

Her body reacted.

Sinking feeling—Belly tightening and heavy legs— Dizzy swirling head—Throat aching— Shoulder sore like a needle pricking me—

She rode back to the castle as fast as she could go.

I must ask them what is wrong with me.

Before she reached the throne room she was overcome by fatigue. She willed herself to climb the steps to her tower room.

So tired-—just want to—

She fell into her bed and slept that day, all day long.

The king and queen sent for the royal doctor and commanded him, "HEAL OUR DAUGHTER."

Some doctors in those days were magicians too and everyone believed they had the power to cure anyone of anything with the right magical ingredients, the right incantations.

The royal doctor-magician began his exam with the traditional questions:

How long has it been— this needing more sleep? What were the first symptoms you noticed? Has anything unusual touched her life?

The king was pacing.

"She has been asking us so many questions just lately."

"She told me her heart flutters and I have noticed such a longing expression on her face," said the queen.

The doctor noticed the princess was staring at a wilted flower. A faint hint of its fragrance drifted to the doctor's nose.

"Aha," said the doctor. "Now we are getting somewhere. This strange flower in her tower bedroom—where did it come from?"

"I don't know," said the king.

"I don't know," said the queen.

Just then the princess opened her eyes and looked into the eyes of the doctor and began to cry.

The doctor questioned her, "Why do you cry? "

"Why do you want to know?"

"She has it," said the doctor. "It's the Questioning Disease, a very bad case of it too. If she isn't confined to her room, it could spread all over the kingdom."

"No, nooo—," said the princess. "I don't want to! You can't shut me up in this tower."

She sat up in her bed.

I should punch that doctor in his nose!

She had to stop herself. She almost did it. The king and queen were frightened.

They had not heard defiance in their daughter's voice before. Rarely had they seen an expression of anger on their daughter's face, and never so many at one time—the frown, a wrinkled brow and half-open slits for eyes, gritted teeth, clenched fists.

The doctor said, "It is a very bad case. There hasn't been a case like this for over a hundred years and if I hadn't lived so long—120 years, this year—the disease might have gone undiagnosed and Castletown might never recover, might never be the same again."

"It's a good thing I come from a long line of healers and that I have a good memory. My grandfather mentioned using the remedy. He told me that there is a valley of horses near where the remedy grows— the remedy for a disease evoked when a princess and a flower awaken together to the whispers of unfinished songs."

When the doctor pronounced that a princess waits for the next note of a responder crystal; that she will recover when one is found; that the crystals grow in the cave of a wizard who lives at the top of a mountain, in a magical valley of horses, the princess lifted her head from her pillow.

"The young man who sells horses knows the way to a valley of horses. He gave me the flower when I fainted, and then I recovered. He was supposed to be here today but he didn't come."

The king sent word to the captain of the guards at all four gates.

"Does the seller of horses come today? Did you see him? Send him to me at once!"

The page, the king's messenger, brought back answers that upset the king.

"Yes, this is the day the horse seller was supposed to come— the eighth day but no, he didn't come through any gate."

The timbre of the doctor's voice changed from sympathetic and confident, to alarmed. He raised his voice and insisted.

"Send word to the guards. Allow the horse seller to enter the gates, no matter what day or hour he might appear there. We must talk to this seller of horses."

There was nothing to do but wait, because no one knew where to find the seller of horses. The very next day a strange thing happened.

The seller of horses appeared at a gate to the walled city on the *ninth* day—with different colored horses.

The guards at the west gate only let the horse seller in because of the orders from the king to do so.

One guard was taunting the horse seller as he was escorting the young man to the throne room.

"You'll never sell any of those horses in Castletown. Don't you know what to bring to Castletown?"

When they finally entered the throne room, the king ran to the horse seller and blurted out.

"The doctor tells me there is a remedy for my daughter's illness in the valley where you get your horses. Even now, the doctor sits at my daughter's bedside, waiting for the remedy."

The horse seller was nervous in the presence of the king. He rubbed the crystal he carried in his pocket—the crystal that fell into his hand, when he was looking at the flower in his cave— the same crystal that rang out such a note of longing that he traveled to Castletown again to see the princess one more time.

Suddenly, the flower in the tower bedroom perked up again and released some of its sweet fragrance. A suggestion of music filled the air.

The crystal in the young man's pocket was sounding overtones. It was responding to the fragrance of the flower.

"What is that sound?" shouted the doctor, as the princess sat up in her bed and then stood up on her own two feet. They followed the tone to the throne room.

A princess looked into a horse seller's eyes again. A poised young man gazed into the eyes of a princess.

The old doctor lowered his voice and almost whispered.

"What is that sound?"

The horse seller answered, "The tone comes from a crystal I carry in my pocket. I found it in a cave above the valley."

"Magical and a miracle!" said the king.

"No, it is knowledge. Any good doctor knows that when a remedy is sought it can be found. Remedies may be found—by a man of my experience—even in the pocket of a horse-seller. This kind of coincidence appears when one is looking for answers. Not a miracle—a benign law of the universe."

The horse seller was forgotten, ignored completely once the princess was herself again.

"Would you like to buy a horse of a different color?" he asked the king.

Everyone laughed at him. The king and queen thought he must be joking. When they understood that he was serious, the king pointed a finger at him.

"Leave and do not come back again unless you have black horses and white horses to sell."

All but the princess thought him foolish. She watched him—looked into his eyes. Something about his eyes fascinated her.

When no one was looking, she whispered in the young man's ear.

"I would like to ride a horse of a different color."

The horse seller whispered to her.

"They are outside the west gate; but you must sew a garment like mine to get outside. I'll come back one more time and if you have a garment like mine, you might, one day, ride a horse of a different color—after you ride a black and white to the valley of horses."

The princess looked long and hard at the horse seller's clothes. There was a strange, uneasy feeling again in her gut.

What am I feeling? What is it—the something whirling, whirling and lifting me up? I could almost fly! What does it mean?

She struggled to keep her poise, to walk slowly away from the castle. It was all she could do to keep from running directly to the dressmaker's shop. After some contrived detours, she finally arrived there.

This time, the princess made no demands, no requests; kept out of sight and watched what the dressmaker did. She watched where the dressmaker kept her tools—the needles and thread and materials she used to make clothes.

Melinda spied the princess out of the corner of her eye but the princess was so very quiet, the dressmaker soon forgot she was there as she worked all day long.

When Melinda was sweeping up threads, folding her materials at the end of the day, the princess slipped out of the shop and walked very slowly back to the castle.

She was tired, so very tired—from trying to learn how to sew. After supper the princess went straight to bed.

That night, she dreamed that she left the castle and returned to the dressmaker's shop. She found some material there. It was just like the material in the horse seller's suit.

She dreamed an eagle came to her—sat on her shoulder and used one of his claws like a needle to sew her a garment just like the horse seller wore.

When the princess woke the next day, sunlight was streaming into her bedroom window warming her face. She glanced up at the clear blue sky, but something dark caught her eye.

Is that an eagle flying away from the castle? I must ask father if he has seen an eagle.

She walked down the steps to the throne room. The dressmaker was there complaining.

"Someone has broken into my shop and stolen materials."

The princess couldn't believe what she was hearing. The dressmaker was almost screaming.

"You are the king! Find whoever is responsible. Do something about it."

The king's whole body was agreeing and rocking back and forth, yes—yes. With his left hand he grabbed both of his own cheeks. He was stroking his cheeks and chin, when he spoke.

"I'll consult my ministers and get back to you."

The princess stayed within hearing distance but out of sight. The king called his ministers together and they sat around a table and harangued among themselves about what could and what should be done.

Finally, late in the afternoon of a long day of nothing but harangues, the king addressed his ministers.

"Enough is enough. Go home. I'll sleep on it. The answer will come to me in the morning."

The ministers were on their way home when the princess stepped into the throne room again.

Should I bother him about my dream about the eagle?

"Father, do you think I might learn how to do something in a dream?"

The king looked up at her.

"I don't know. I use the wisdom of today and trust my ministers for good advice. Sometimes after a good rest, the mind clears. But I do not remember when a dream solved a kingly problem. You aren't coming down with that disease again; are you?"

There were raised eye brows on his kingly face. He was stroking his chin again.

"No, noooo–I was just thinking about a silly dream I had last night," the princess said.

That night, when the princess slept, she dreamed she returned to the dressmaker's shop and left three gold coins where she found the material in her dream the night before.

The next morning the horse seller appeared again at the north gate with just a very few black horses and one white horse.

The princess heard the gate open. She stood up to look out her watch tower window.

Oh–NO! I don't have it. Not enough time–

All of sudden she noticed it.

Something soft and lumpy against my foot—

17

She sat down on her bed again and pulled it out. There was a garment under the bed, just like the horse seller's garment!

The princess snatched it up and took it with her. She was running down the castle steps in such a hurry she didn't stop to wonder. As she tiptoed past the throne room she heard a commotion in there. The dressmaker was thanking the king for solving her problem.

"You are a generous and wise king and only a royal person such as yourself could find such a royal solution."

The king wisely kept silent and just listened as the dressmaker spoke about *Gold Coins!*

"Three gold coins were there in my shop this morning, in the place of the stolen material."

The king was astonished but he just listened and waited. The dressmaker stopped speaking. She was waiting for his reply.

Finally he said, "Yes, yeeees—of course, of course, that's what kings do."

Then he waved her away and leaned back into his throne and pondered.

I must have some unknown magical powers; after all, I did declare that the answer would present itself to me in the morning.

The princess kept on tiptoeing past the throne room and right out of the castle. She held the garment out for the horse seller to see but then she stopped—stopped and wondered and looked at the miraculous garment she carried.

The horse seller smiled at her and winked. He whispered.

"You have the garment. Put it on. Mount my trusty steed. Ride out through the west gate. Wave to the guard and I will meet you there, outside the gate."

The princess hid in the corner between the castle and her own watch tower as she changed garments. The horse seller was behind the royal stables, painting white spots on a black horse.

When the painting was done, the horse seller took the few blacks and one white he had to sell around to the front of the royal stables. The princess smiled as she heard him.

"My horses are a bargain; the best gold coins can buy. Even now one of the royal family rides one of my horses."

The princess was riding through the west gate as the horse seller sold his last horse. His painted horse was now dry enough to mount.

The horse seller rode a newly black and whited steed out the east gate of Castletown. The sun was beginning to set in the west as the horse seller circled right and right again and then motioned to the princess—heading west—to stay directly ahead of him.

The guard at the west gate was squinting, blinking his eyes in the sun.

Two horse sellers riding west. No! Couldn't be. Sun in my eyes plays tricks.

The young man and the princess rode on and on into the sun. Just as the sun was setting they galloped into the foothills of mountains and disappeared from sight.

At the foot of a mountain they came to thick underbrush that concealed a hidden opening in the side of the mountain.

There was a kind of deep crack that led down and around and deeper and deeper into the ground. As they disappeared into the ground the horse seller dismounted his horse. He patted it on the rump.

"My horse carries the supplies I have purchased into the valley. Our horses will find refreshment on their own way home tonight while we sleep."

He stood beside the princess and helped her dismount, and then he freed her horse too. The two fugitives from Castletown proceeded on foot down the ever darkening path and as the path disappeared, the princess became more and more anxious. She was shaking with fear.

The crystal in the young man's pocket began to vibrate with a sympathetic note. He cradled it gently in his hand until its one note woke rocks inside the mountain and then he spoke.

"The mountain sings a comforting song to us now. Listen, you can hear it!"

Leave fears behind you. Fears won't find you. Behind you—won't find you—Find you.

She heard the notes and almost understood the words but was more assured by his smile. He looked down at his feet and rubbed his shins.

"I remember skinning my shins; I was alone and still, I survived my own dreadful mountain climbing times and then I found this hidden passageway. It's the only way I know from here to the valley of horses. Listen to the mountain's pulses comforting us, urging us on. Together we'll find magic. It is waiting for us to catch up to it."

Just as she thought they were only getting deeper and deeper into trouble, they came to what looked like the bottom of a dry well. He whispered.

"We'll rest here for the night."

His whisper echoed around and around in the well like a lullaby.

Rest—here for the night. Here—for the night— rest—Here rest— Here—here—

A weary and shaken princess fell asleep in a horse seller's arms.

Prophecy

Back in Castletown, the king questioned the guards.

"What did you see?"

One guard said, "I saw the princess talking to the horse seller but then I lost track of her–don't remember seeing her again."

"What about the horse-seller? Has he gone?"

Two guards, said at once, "Yes, he left by my gate. He was riding his black and white horse."

The east and west guards looked at one another and were astonished. The king's mouth dropped open and he spoke with a groan.

"That is impossible but today seems to be a strange day with impossible things happening. Ride to both horizons. Find them. Bring the princess back to us."

A tear threatened to escape the king's eye. He tried to brush the moisture away with the back of his hand.

How can I tell my queen that our daughter cannot be found?

The east guard searched east, always riding east. He searched by moonlight and all the next day but he just traveled deeper and deeper into the desert. There was nothing on the horizon when he turned back to the castle.

The west guard rode west until his way was lit by moonlight, until he came to thick underbrush at the foothills of mountains. He camped there until daylight and then searched again.

As he finally turned around to go back to the castle, he was complaining to his horse.

"Everyone knows there is no way over or around these mountains."

And then he heard it.

A musical sound coming from the mountain.

He dismounted to put his ear to the ground but suddenly he was staggered. The ground was moving and the horse reared up in fright. He grabbed the reins, barely managed to mount his horse and gallop back to the safety of castle and king.

As he approached the gate to Castletown he looked back at where he had been and he was amazed that he had escaped what was behind him—the enormous rift developing in the sand.

A rolling, rumbling woke the princess. She was lying in the strong arms of a mysterious man she hardly knew and yet longed to know. Something welled up in her chest—seemed to rise from below her belly.

It felt like a pulsing, a going around and around, that rose higher and higher and reached to her heart. The pulsing elicited a wistful tender feeling she had not known before. Suddenly she wanted to kiss the stranger.

Just then he woke and kissed her on the forehead.

"We have far to go to the valley of horses and we must go quickly now. The stones sing a warning song."

I can't believe I am here in his arms. Am I awake or sleeping?

She was struggling to regain some sense of where she was and how she had come to this place.

"What are you saying? What am I doing here? Where are the horses?"

"The horses gather in the secret valley. Hold my hand and we'll be there soon."

He led her around the bottom of the well.

We're just going around in circles—climbing, climbing, and getting nowhere.

Around and around they went.

Dizzy—Queasy— I could slip or fall.

She was looking down at where they had been. Her footsteps were faltering. She was beginning to doubt the wisdom of her decision to leave Castletown.

He stopped for a few moments, smiled at her and put his arm around her shoulders and gave her an encouraging squeeze.

The path finally straightened out and she saw up ahead—what looked like a light at the end of a tunnel. On and on they went until they emerged into a cave at the top of the mountain. They stepped into sunlight at the front of the cave and looked down.

Horses, a whole valley full of horses!

It was then that the ledge they were standing on shook. The floor of the cave buckled and seemed to rise and fall. Rocks tumbled. They clung to one another and backed away from the edge of the ledge.

What is this fearful rumbling?

The ledge was holding– not crumbling. They were still standing on rock solid footing. The princess sat down on a huge boulder and tapped her eyebrow—close to her nose—and tapped beside her eye— away from her nose—and then under her eye.

With two fingers she was tapping under her nose, in the crease of her chin. With four fingers she was tapping on her chest under her arm. With her fist she was tapping at the base of her neck. The horse seller stared at her.

"What are you doing?"

She kept on tapping, tapping the ends of her fingers—close to the fingernail. She was saying something to herself. Finally she stopped tapping.

"Don't you know about the healing buttons? I have never been so frightened and so I just tapped all the healing buttons I could remember."

"What were you saying? What do you mean healing buttons?" he asked her.

She didn't say anything for a few minutes. She was staring down and to the left as if she were remembering a feeling. It was a childhood fear—that gasping, choking she endured when she was about two.

Suddenly she felt it again. Fearful images flooded back to her in a rush.

Tripping, falling head first into a bucket of water—

She tapped again.

"Even though I was clumsy and fell into trouble and frightened myself it turned out all right. I accept myself and that I am afraid sometimes. I can go on. It will be all right."

Finally she sighed. She took a deep breath and cleared her throat and then she spoke softly to the horse seller.

"I remember screaming every time the page hauling water from our well came close to me."

She told the horse seller what she was remembering. That one day, when she told her grandmother she was afraid of falling into the water. Her grandmother hugged her and said, "I know that tummy-tight feeling . It's time to *use the healing buttons.*"

The princess tried to explain her tapping to the horse seller:

Tapping on the side of my hand and under my eye and under my nose—while saying, even though I have this fear of water in a bucket, I deeply and completely accept myself— activated the healing buttons.

Grandmother and I tapped together and then I tapped again saying, *I am bigger now and I don't stumble and fall into buckets. Little children learn from their stumbles.*

I was feeling better but we tapped again about the choking and gasping before grandmother told me to dip a cup into the bucket and bring us a refreshing drink of water. I didn't hesitate. The bucket no longer frightened me.

The horse seller said, "A few minutes ago, I thought I heard you saying, *This tightness, this fear.*"

The princess nodded.

"Yes, that's right—so the healing buttons would know how to help me, here."

There was a slight quaver in his voice that drew her to him.

"It's hard to admit it but I'm not breathing easy. I'm holding my breath and gritting my teeth and I'm still a little shaken."

He was quiet for a few moments. She took his hand in hers and tapped on the outside edge of his palm.

She said, "Repeat after me: Even though I have this fear of losing my footing, I deeply and completely accept myself."

She continued her tapping on the outside edge of his palm and together, they said those words three times.

And then she tapped at the beginning of his eyebrow, at the outside edge of his eye, under his eye.

"this fear–"

and under his nose—

"this fear"

and on his chin at the crease under his lips—

"this fear"

and where the neck meets the chest—

"this fear"

He stammered and then almost shouted.

"What? How? I am feeling better already."

She tapped under his arm.

"Any remaining fear"

and then the top of his head and both wrists,

"any remaining fear."

She looked at the relieved horse seller and said, "One day, one of grandmother's favorite young knights was hesitant to enter the jousting arena. She helped him overcome his fear, this way."

The horse seller gathered a princess in his arms and hugged her. He whispered in her ear.

"Thank you. Now I know we can get through anything together. But, you may not be able to go home again. The mountain has a mind of its own. I did warn you that our journey together would have dangers."

Back at the castle, a mystery grew and rumors flew. Some connected the disappearance of the princess to the horse seller but no one could or would say for sure what happened.

The guards at the East and West gates squelched any suggestion that the princess could have slipped by them.

Many nights the king lay awake tossing and turning, ruminating.

Wanting to choose her own clothes, it was a clue. If only I had known my daughter better, if only I had listened more closely to what she was saying, I might have had some idea. We sensed some danger to her. Why didn't I do more than tell the guards to watch her when the horse seller was inside our walls?

Why didn't I tell her how much she means to me? Why didn't I keep an eye on her myself? Why couldn't I keep her safe from danger behind our walls? Why? Why?

The ground shook and continued to shake for days after the princess disappeared. Huge cracks appeared in the floor of the desert. Fire and smoke spewed from the mountain range in the west.

The king called his ministers together and shouted.

"Explain to me what has happened. What is happening?"

One of the king's wisest ministers carefully unrolled some fragments of scripture written on—up until then an almost forgotten scroll.

He looked the king in the eye, straightened his shoulders and reminded him.

"It is tattered and soiled. There are tears and words missing in this ancient scroll but it seems to me we have come to the time foretold in it."

He began to read the words out loud:

once upon a rhyme		*royalty*	
steps over the line.		*disappears*	*lost*
place	*changes*	*reveals unknown, forgotten*	

energies Tapping overcomes a fear.   sign of twice upon
a time draws   near.   Unveiling   rift   desert
sands   shift   A sacred rock   path will split
ageless age conspires   fulfills desires   smoke and fires
wizard   shard.   Time twists a braided vine
princess wears a common design   fountain   mountain,
sacred task   flask uncorked again   sum where, when
majesty will see   a scroll unfolds   what fits
the mold   earth bubbling up   boulders fill
an empty cup   treasures   find   the right
way   measures for a mind, today   Be stirred   not
shaken   path not taken   waken to the core   restored
once more   the leap through dimensions   sacred
intentions   find inside rhymes   Thrice or more
upon sum times
*   cork   flying pyramid   quark*

He had been holding the scroll up with one hand, unrolling it with his other hand. Now he rolled it up again, took a deep breath, let his shoulders drop and raised his voice .

It may sound like nonsense but I'm sure it's much more than what it seems. It reminds me of some other fragments I found that look like prescriptions or forgotten formulas we once knew how to use.

No one scroll, no matter how sacred, how ancient, is long enough, complete enough to give us all the answers. We can't hold all the answers in our hand and yet there is a kind of wisdom here—missing words or not.

Perhaps the scroll unrolls us—points to what is still concealed. Perhaps we must seek for our missing princess in another dimension. The scroll says you have the eyes to see, Your Majesty.

The king shook his head in agreement but was not consoled. He did not voice the nagging thoughts that haunted him.

She must be with the horse seller. He knows how to cross the desert. But could he protect her from the unexpected eruptions—the fires, the treacherous rift in the sands?

There was an air of expectation and hesitation in the kingdom for many moons but nothing unusual happened. The queen refused to give up the search for her daughter. Searching continued on and on and threatened to disrupt Castletown life until finally, the king declared in a written proclamation:

Forever after, but just once a year,
on this day of disappearances,
We shall stop what we are doing.
We shall conduct a search for what is
lost. The day shall be called Precious.

The custom of celebrating holidays was begun. Rumblings in the mountains ceased. Life behind secure, defended walls was the same, day after day.

The king unrolled the ancient scroll again and again but the mysterious words never did enlighten him. Every time the earth rumbled the king wondered if the earth had swallowed up his princess. On those days tears rolled down his cheeks.

The words written on the scroll were beginning to fade and the scroll was beginning to crumble. The king's minister finally persuaded the king to give him the scroll for safe keeping. It was rolled up, sealed in a jar and hidden again in a royal archive cave.

Valley Secrets

Rocks were no longer raining from the roof of the cave. Rumbling and jolting of the mountain had ceased. She was standing on a narrow ledge, at the mouth of that cave in the rocky face of a mountain, staring into a hidden, forbidden valley and she was gathering her wits about her.

Memory or dream? Too vivid—couldn't be dreaming again. Nooo–, after a short but very sound sleep I wakened snuggled into the warmth of the horse seller's body. When I opened my eyes, it looked like we were in a deep dry well.

I can't believe we escaped from Castletown—eluded my father's guards. Daybreak—there was enough light to see him, sleeping beside me; stirring, opening his eyes, looking into my eyes. He did kiss me. I am not dreaming.

An unknown rhythm was roused in her body as she was remembering his voice urging her on:

The earth is speaking in rumbles, telling us to hurry to the hidden valley of horses. We must begin now, at once! Hold my hand. Not far, but a very steep climb—

She looked at her clothes, at the horse seller's clothes.

*We **are** dressed alike. That's how we slipped thru the gates. Setting sun blinded the guard at the west gate. He had no way of knowing that I was going.*

At first glance it might have been difficult to tell them apart. The princess had straight, long silky golden hair and the horse seller had long blonde hair too. His hair was naturally wavy. He was just a little bit taller, just a little bit broader.

She lingered over her thoughts about the horse seller, about her escape.

He held my hand, pulled me up from my slumbering and pointed. Then I could see the spiraling steep path ahead of us. He brought me to this dangerous and exciting place–to this cave, to this ledge.

His whispers were so sweet. How did he say it?

"When I first brought the black and white horses from this valley to sell in Castletown, I didn't guess that I might meet a princess and then when I did meet you, I didn't dare hope that you might, one day, accompany me to this lost, secret, almost forgotten, hidden valley of horses."

Tears came to her eyes as she remembered.

Mother, father, castle, my beautiful clothes—left behind to ride a horse of a different color.

The mountain rumbled and grumbled again. She was looking down, beginning to feel dizzy and afraid. The horse seller's encouraging words came back to her.

Keep on going. Look up to the light. Don't look back; don't look down. You can do it.

Her legs felt like they might not hold her up. She thought her knees might buckle. She sat down on a flat rock and leaned back against another rock. She was trembling all over.

She tapped her chest, the side of her hand. She was rubbing the sore spot by her collar bone. She was almost shouting.

"Even though there is nothing but a dark hole behind us, I deeply and completely accept myself. Even though I don't know where I'm going, I made a good decision. Even though I don't know where I'm going, everything will turn out all right."

She was rolling her eyes around in a circle to the right—looking at the roof of the cave and then the floor. And then she was rolling her eyes around again, but to the left.

He was watching her tap her healing buttons and roll her eyes. She sighed and then was quiet, just sitting there.

He asked her, "Why do you roll your eyes?"

She raised her shoulders toward her ears and gestured with one hand—palm up as if weighing something.

"Grandmother told me it balances a person's brain—a person's thinking."

The horse seller was quiet, pondering.

I wonder if it is anything like centering?

He patted her on the shoulder .

"My grandmother taught me how to find peace inside myself and she called it centering. She said if you just take a few deep breaths and pay attention to your breaths, you will come back to a safe place inside yourself."

"She told me to—count to four as you breathe in; hold your breath for another count of four. Breathe out to the count of eight. Hold your breath again to the count of four and then breathe naturally again."

The princess tried a centering breath to calm her inner voice that kept questioning her.

What am I caught up in? Is this daydreaming—going over these things, retracing my steps, again and again? Why?

Why can't I believe it's really happening to me? It has to be real I can feel it—the unrelenting cold hard rock, I'm sitting on.

She blinked a few tears from her eyes. She blinked again as a beam of sunlight pierced the settling dust.

She reached out to touch the horse seller, to make sure that he was really there. He grasped her hand and helped her up. They stood close together, as far out on the ledge of that rocky barren mountain as they could to see his verdant world.

It seemed to go on and on forever, far below them. What was a familiar sight to him was strange, and exciting to her—a foreign world to explore.

Horses, a whole valley of horses were running wild and free, beautiful horses, many different colors of horses, in a valley carpeted velvety green.

It wasn't long before there was another sharp jolt and this time a rolling sensation under their feet. They were staggered at the edge of the cliff and almost lost their balance as the earth shifted and filled in the back of the cave with boulders. She looked over her shoulder at the space that was left—that now looked like a huge tea cup to her.

No way back and maybe soon, no more cave, nothing to do but go on.

She was clinging to him as they regained their balance and took a few tentative steps onto the path down the mountain. He had one arm around her. He pointed at the horses below.

"The wizard and the horses come and go places I have yet to know. Perhaps they'll lead us to another way. Perhaps there is another way back to Castletown."

Hand in hand, they were on their way— on the path he knew to the valley.

They had only taken a few steps when the princess paused and looked at the horse seller.

"What is your name, horse seller?"

He stopped, didn't say anything; looked down at the horses and then stared out into space. A tear trickled out of his right eye. He was looking up to the left. She nudged him.

"It has been such a long time since anyone called me by name. Grandmother called me, *Dreamer*, as we sat by the fire, in the fireplace inside her castle."

His eyes dropped a little. His voice took on a gentle quiet tone.

"She used to say: *Come to me, Dreamer, with heart of a lion, It is story telling time.* She told me stories—stories about wild and tame animals in the kingdom. Her cricket story brought me to this wondrous place and another of her stories may have saved my life, *here*, in this lost valley."

The princess cuddled up to Dreamer, laid her head on his shoulder for a moment and then took his hand.

"My grandmother told me stories too. She warned me about wolves. Did your grandmother tell you any stories about wolves?"

"Yes, stories, with warnings, and with wisdom in them. She led me to believe wild animals can be instructors for the very wise."

Precious yawned. "What was her name? What did she tell you?"

"The horse seller cleared his throat. My grandmother was called Fair Maiden and I loved her, *Once upon a time, it seems like yesterday stories,* and especially this wolf story about a pack of wolves who lived in the woods surrounding our castle."

Wolves are curious animals and most times, if they are not hungry, they are not dangerous. You can learn to be like them. When anyone new or a strange animal stumbles into their territory, they run off a little ways and sit down and quiet themselves and use their senses to sniff the air, to test the ground, to listen for unusual sounds.

"Remembering this part of her story may have saved my life."

Wolves usually kill what they must to survive and no more. But sometimes after a hard winter, wolf habits are not predictable. They can go into a frenzy and kill and attack and attack and kill, much more than they can eat.

"Even so, she said, we can learn to love wolves."

The horse seller was silent for a few minutes before he spoke about what he was remembering:

Grandmother had fun with horses too—played games with them. She used to whistle for Topper, her favorite horse. No matter what that horse was doing, or how far into the pasture he was, he would stop and look at her and then they would race to the stable.

One day I told her: I want to find the magical valley, the valley the cricket told you is behind impenetrable mountains.

She said, *"Remember, about wolves when you get there. Use all your senses and be quiet enough to hear a cricket."*

"How did that save your life?" asked the princess.

They were not noticing how far they had come down the mountain path, how late it was in the day. His stories seemed to carry her—to put wings on her feet.

He was losing track of time and place—gazing into her attentive eyes.

"It was a long time ago. I was just exploring, wasn't thinking about grandmother's story. I noticed a ledge across a crevasse. I

33

couldn't help wondering—*ledge and a broken staircase on the side of the mountain—* "

Finally I decided to make my way across that crevasse even though the staircase looked like it didn't go anywhere. I climbed around and over boulders. I fell several times, climbing up to another ledge on my side of the crevasse.

What a jumping off place—a short distance to the other side but the very deep crevasse was intimidating. I balanced myself carefully— took deep breaths and counted them until I was calm, until I felt feet and legs ready to go.

I kept my eyes on the staircase and when I was ready, I jumped. Loose rocks under my feet started to give way. I grabbed onto a scrub bush growing out of the side of the mountain.

Huge rocks tumbled into the chasm. I held on and swung my legs to one side of the bush. My feet touched ground. I was almost afraid to put my whole weight on the narrowing ledge.

I was still trembling as I reached one hand over my head and finally took hold of the staircase. I pulled myself up onto it and then climbed and climbed, until I was nowhere.

I was tired, hungry, angry, and lonesome. I was stuck somewhere between a deep crevasse and the shale of a slippery, steep slope above the ledge—still over my head.

I was thinking: *There's no way to get over that mountain and no way back. Yet somehow, I know I will make it.*

I was dressed very much like we are dressed in dark and sturdy clothes suitable for mountain climbing so I was at least protected from the cold mountain breezes that were blowing. But, wearing those clothes, I blended into the side of the mountain. It would have been very difficult for anyone to find me, if anyone were looking for me.

I was on the last rung (the top of the staircase was ladder-like) when I remembered the wolf story.

I was quiet and used all my senses to sense what I could about where I was. I caught a glimpse of a huge, beautiful but also monstrous black bird overhead. The bird dived down, down, and around, closer and closer to me.

It was three, maybe four times larger than I am. I didn't move. Didn't blink an eye. The bird sat down on a narrow ledge of outcropping rock, just over my head. Out of the side of my eye I could see gigantic talons curled over rock.

We both sat there quietly for I don't know how long when I noticed a movement in its feathers and I sensed a lifting of its wings. I don't know how or why I did it but I let go of the rung and stood up at the top of that ladder. I balanced myself and stretched and reached out as far as I could.

One hand touched and then grabbed hold of the leg of that bird. It flew off with me hanging onto it. I was dangling in mid-air. I couldn't scream for fear the bird might notice me. I had no idea what might become of me.

Up, up we rose, higher and higher. We soared past the peak. The bird spread its wings and sailed around and around with the wind currents generated by the mountains.

I closed my eyes for a moment. I was afraid I was losing my grip. When I opened my eyes again, I saw it— this beautiful valley of horses beneath us.

Where I had been stuck, at the top of the ladder, was nowhere in sight. The bird flew toward a cave in the mountain and just before it closed its wings, I let go.

It sat down on (He pointed.) that very ledge. I landed on another ledge beneath its cave. I crouched and hugged the side of the mountain and went on until I found the cave we just left. The bird didn't seem to know I was there.

When I was safely inside the cave, I sat very still and found myself wondering: *Perhaps I have learned how to disappear, how to make myself invisible or perhaps the bird is blind to human beings. I must be like grandmother and learn all I can about this creature and about this strange place. When that bird is hungry, I don't want to be in its sight.*

I was wondering about winter coming and if birds like this go into frenzy after a hard winter. I knew I must find a safe place to hide from it. I sat quietly; I sniffed the air. There was a fragrance like fresh fruit. I followed my nose to one side of the cliff.

Staying close to the side of the mountain I found a winding path. It looked like it might go all the way down to the valley of horses. The path was wide at first but it grew narrower and when I turned one corner, there was an apple tree growing in the middle of that grass carpeted narrowing path.

It looked like an old apple tree. Branches were gnarled and twisted and the tree itself was decaying but it still held apples. I was hungry so I ate some. I sat down to rest under the tree and fell asleep as the sun was setting and shining in my eyes.

When I woke up the sun was overhead and blazing hot. My head was leaning against the trunk of a tree. I was in a clearing made by rotting wormy apple droppings and fallen twigs and branches.

Wafts of cider, vinegar, and wine came to me. I couldn't see a path into or out of this clearing. It was hard to see ahead to where I might be going because chest-high field grasses surrounded the clearing.

The grasses looked like a swaying, marching in place army, standing guard, laying siege to the place where I was sleeping. Suddenly, I remembered: *It was short and lush–the grass, like soft carpet when I lay down.*

I was confused, afraid, and looking around for the path I had been walking on. Saw-grasses grabbed at my clothes and cut my flesh as I stumbled away from the tree.

I almost stepped over a cliff. One foot was in mid-air *when* grandmother's wolf story came to me. I sat down. I tested the ground.

"The next step—how close I had come to taking it. It would have been my last step. I might have missed so much–my wondrous adventure here, meeting you and our journey together."

I inched myself along, feeling first and then taking stock, going on when I could, taking a few steps, standing up, looking around, sitting down, resting and then testing again—not able to see where I was or where I was going.

I was looking for a way to break out of my confinement—looking for a bigger picture. Finally, I broke out of over-grown thistles and nettles and tangled grasses and found a bearable, wearable path again. Still, it was steep and rugged with uneven-ups and downs.

I struggled to go on and to keep from slipping, and back-sliding. Finally I made it over some kind of hump. My feet found solid ground again. It was such a relief.

I ran down this inviting path until I was almost out of breath. I had to stop for a few minutes. I looked up to see how far and where I had come from.

Then I saw it again. It was here and very near—that hideous, huge bird diving, gliding, landing on the path I had just traveled. Something golden on the path was glinting against a dark grey strata of mountain rocks.

I heard a horrible scream. Talons and the bird's beak were hooked into whatever it was. The path turned red and then the bird flew off to its cave.

I was thinking: *Its head looks like a human head. No, it must be the thin air up here or the glare of reflected sunlight that distorts its image.*

My grandmother's words about being able to love wolves came back to me and I wondered if I could ever love that monstrous bird— its black feathers shimmering blue and green and purple in the sun.

I reminded myself: *Eating habits—I must observe the bird's habits to learn to survive in this strange place.*

I climbed back up the path to get closer to the bird. There was no getting around the blood on the path. I had to walk through it to observe the bird. The smell of its slaughter was in my nose as I got closer and closer to its cave.

My clothes, almost the color of barren mountain rock still hid me. The bird took no notice of me. I grew bolder and crept closer and closer. I was almost beside it when I saw its feathers move, sensed the lift of a wing.

I reached up and I grabbed onto one of its legs again as it was taking off. We flew higher and higher and higher and then suddenly, down, down, down to the floor of the valley of horses, to a peaceful wide river flowing thru the valley.

As the bird was folding its wings to land, I jumped off and landed on a horse. The bird drank and bathed itself in the river. It sat down in shallow water, spread and dipped its wings and then shook the water off.

I was watching it, trying to keep track of the bird and at the same time, holding onto a bucking horse. It was trying to throw me off—running away from the river and the Sharpie.

"What is a Sharpie?" asked the princess.

"That's the bird's name," Dreamer answered her.

"How do you know?"

"The horse told me."

"It said: *Get off my back. A Sharpie is not known for bestowing anything good in this valley.*"

I tried to reassure the horse.

" I am not bestowed by a Sharpie. I just caught hold of its leg and rode here unnoticed by the bird."

Needless to say I was very surprised to hear a horse talking and he was surprised to hear from a package dropped out of the sky.

It was hard for him to believe that this strange someone, once so close to a Sharpie was not dangerous. To calm him I began to tell him a once upon a time story about my grandmother, Fair Maiden—that she taught me to be wily as a wolf and as wise as a grandmother. The horse interrupted me.

"Fair Maiden— that name sounds so familiar. I remember a cricket once told me a story about a fair maiden held captive in her own father's castle. I thought it was just another story the cricket made up to keep us entertained in our secret box canyon—to keep us calm on long cold winter nights, so we wouldn't stray till spring came again and the Sharpie was well fed. Is it really a true story?"

"It sounds like, it might be the story my grandmother, Fair Maiden, told me," I said to the horse.

Just then, the princess interrupted Dreamer's story. She grabbed his arm and pointed to a huge black bird soaring above them. It glistened and reflected beautiful colors from its black feathers. Dreamer hugged the princess.

"That's it, the Sharpie. We are safe for now. Its eyes are only half open. I have learned from living with it in this valley that when its eyes are half open, it has just eaten and is in some kind of stupor."

" I have been lucky catching my rides with it when it isn't aware of much that is going on around it. We must find the path down the mountain before dark. There's a young orchard grown up around an old apple tree. Stay close. Beyond the apple tree the path divides. We'll take the inside path, the cave path. There are some other inviting paths but I know this one is safe."

"I am so hungry," said the princess. "Let's eat some apples."

They started down the path and when they came to the orchard, Dreamer said, "I have an uneasy feeling in the pit of my stomach."

"You are just hungry. I'm, hungry too and tired and I will be angry if we don't stop to rest and eat," she insisted.

She ran to a tree, picked an apple, sat down under the tree and leaned back and took a bite.

Dreamer heard her say, "My eyelids are so heavy."

Dreamer thought he remembered something but he didn't know what it was. He bit into an apple too. He was so tired. He sat down next to her and fell asleep on the soft green grass carpet.

The ground was rumbling when the princess and Dreamer woke up. He was suddenly afraid.

"We must hurry to the cave. There is no telling how long we have been sleeping here or what season it is and whether or not we are in danger from the Sharpie."

The princess said, with a tone of irritation in her voice, "Surely you are mistaken. It is morning and we have had a good sleep. You must be still dreaming."

"No, you wake up," Dreamer said. "Look around you. The grass is tinged with red and it has grown to mid-calf. When we went to sleep it was green and short as a carpet."

They both stood up and Dreamer led the way to a small cave almost hidden by brush. At the back of the cave there was an opening onto a path that branched out in three different directions. At the junction of the three paths there was an upright black stone. As they set foot on the path they were going to take, the ground rumbled again and a crack appeared in that path. The horse seller didn't just step over it. He stopped and looked and looked again.

"This black stone reminds me—one day grandmother heard an elderly wolf tell a pack of young ones a strange story."

"Do you really think she could hear a wolf story?" asked the princess.

"Yes, I believe. No, I know she could. She told me what the elder wolf said."

Sniff this place well. It smells like another time and place, a place where three paths come together and where there is an upright black stone. A princess and a stranger will come to a parting of the ways there.

It is a sacred place we elders recognize—the place of sudden shifts in the ground. Wolf lore teaches us it can be a dangerous place, at the time of separation.

We know to watch for cracks and depressions that might be developing. When that time comes, only a real princess can heal what is broken. She must choose to jump forth and back and forth again to repair the path.

Dreamer looked into disbelieving princess eyes, as he continued the story.

Grandmother said the baby wolves howled and then nuzzled one another and shook their ears as if to say they couldn't believe what she was telling them. It is my belief that we have come to that time, that place.

All the while Dreamer was telling the princess the story, the crack on their path was widening. He was looking at her expectantly.

She shook her head and said, "I am afraid, afraid and not a good jumper. Why is it getting wider and wider? It sounds like a crazy story to me. I didn't know your grandmother. It might just be a coincidence."

"You must take a chance and jump," Dreamer said as he jumped across the crack in the path.

He kept calling out encouraging words to her. He didn't know she couldn't hear him. She looked so lost and confused–on the other side of the crack, just standing there and staring into space.

He tried to jump back across the crack to her but there was an invisible barrier.

The princess was dismayed and all alone on her side of the crack.

I must be having a dream. This couldn't be real. Dreamer couldn't just disappear.

The ground was shaking her, urging her to make up her mind. She almost lost her balance as the crack widened again.

She whispered to herself.

"I don't know what to do. It can't be true. How can a person repair a crack in the ground? I'm afraid! I'm alone!"

She thought she heard her grandmother's voice.

"Tap your arms together at the wrists. Tap your chest and the top of your head."

She tapped. Her thoughts cleared.

No, he is here. I was holding Dreamer's hand. He has to be there on the other side of the crack and I want to ride a horse of a different color.

She was holding her breath as she jumped across a chasm right into the arms of that Dreamer—that strange handsome young man with the fascinating eyes.

"You disappeared when you jumped to the other side," she scolded. "And I was alone and afraid."

"I didn't know. I tried to reach you again but there was an invisible barrier. I just waited for you to make the jump. I knew we would get back together again because of what my grandmother told me."

You will journey with another someone. It is meant to be. You will have exciting, mysterious adventures together.

"Let's hurry down our path," the princess urged.

Dreamer wouldn't go and almost shouted, "NO!"

And then he said more gently.

"No, Princess, some parts of the wolf tale are missing but grandmother's stories are true. What was lost from the story–what we couldn't know was that you wouldn't hear me or see me on the other side of the crack. Some things even a grandmother doesn't know."

"If the crack isn't repaired, we might lose three pathways and this cave and then, we may not be safe from the Sharpie. You must jump back and forth again to repair the path—to fulfill the story."

"I don't want to, don't want to, don't want to," the princess said in a pouting, wheedling tone of voice.

"I don't want to leave you—don't want to be alone. I don't want to wonder if this is all a dream."

Dreamer looked down at the crack. Tears filled his eyes.

There was a catch in the princess' throat, a tightening up feeling. Her nose was crinkling.

Why is he crying? I'm going to cry too. Tears running out of my eyes.

She put one hand on the top of her head and tapped— one hand on her belly. Her arms dropped to her sides. She took a deep breath, reached out and jumped, back and forth across the ever widening crack without thinking any more about it.

Earth rumbled. Their path snapped back together again. Dreamer hugged the princess and instructed her.

"We'll have to be wily as wolves, courageous as mother bears who find a safe cave, who sleep and wake up to playful newborn cubs. For us too, there will be new responsibilities, unforeseen adventures."

"Our life here must be as natural as this place, as natural as the horses you came to ride if we are to find our way out of this valley again."

Dreamer reached down and plucked a flower from the path and handed it to the princess. It sang just one note of longing, almost the same note she heard in her bedroom, in the castle. It seemed so long ago now.

The responder crystal Dreamer carried in his pocket answered with another note in the song of the valley of horses.

"When will I ride a horse of a different color?" asked the princess.

Dreamer, the horse seller shook his head. "When it agrees to carry you."

They were walking hand in hand, when Dreamer asked, "What is your name, princess?"

"My given name is Pearlynnaline, but I remember my grandmother, my father's mother, called me, Precious."

As Dreamer and Precious descended together, they were unaware of the shadow that crossed their path—of the silent danger gliding overhead.

Magic Bed

Precious and Dreamer were finding their way down a narrow rock strewn mountain path to the valley of horses. Night was beginning to fall. Shadows grew longer and their footsteps shorter. The pace slowed. They held hands. They gazed into one another's eyes. The light on the path was becoming dimmer.

A monstrous bird, the dreadful murderous Sharpie had been disturbed by rumblings in the mountain. Its eyes opened wide with fright. It spread gigantic wings and began to soar with the mountain air currents.

Not hungry but I must remember where it is, that something golden—at least another mouthful.

Golden meant food to the bird. As it circled it caught a glimpse of sun on blonde hair, just a glint against the grey mountain.

Unaware of the danger circling overhead, a princess was telling Dreamer:

My grandmother said I was like a gift from an unfathomably deep sea, a mysterious place of salty waters. Before Ynnaline was lost, before we built the walls, caravan travelers on the way to the sea, sometimes refreshed themselves at Castletown. One caravan traveler, a wealthy merchant gave my grandmother a sea shell that came from water, called ocean.

"This ocean is deep and as wide—no, much wider than the desert surrounding your castle," he said to my grandmother.

Grandmother said she was checking out my tiny toes when I was born. One toenail, the toenail on my right big toe looked like a sea shell the traveler showed her.

Sea shells come from ocean water and water is precious in the desert.

When that thought came to her, she decided to call me, Precious.

Grandmother said a few days before I was born my father was given a pearl by a visiting emissary from another kingdom. Only gifts of great value were exchanged in the desert and so my father named me, Pearl but mother said Pearl was too short a name for royalty and so she added Ynnaline—a medicine formulated long ago by ancient wizards and sorceresses.

You are named so that you will remember and one day find the healing magic given to your grandmother.

I remember her words. My mother saying that to me so many times. So long ago–

My grandmother used to sing me to sleep, singing a mysterious ancient lullaby. She said grandmothers had been singing it to babies long before the gift was given, long before it was lost. I can still hear her singing it to me—that ancient cradle song.

Sleep baby sleep, sleep baby sleep
Somewhere in the down deep
a mysterious mountain
a dreamer's fountain
and near its source a talking horse
Somewhere in the down deep
sleep baby sleep
A silent foal with one red eye
comes by and by
and leads you to your goal
Somewhere in the down deep

Sleep baby sleep
Near an echoing sound
what is lost is found
Sleep baby sleep
Somewhere in the down deep
dry tears are not tragic
a sign post to magic
Sleep baby sleep
Somewhere in the down deep
Grandmother is near
and you are safe from fear
Sleep baby sleep, sleep baby sleep

"Well, Precious, there is a talking horse in this valley," said Dreamer. "And it talks to me."

"Could an ancient lullaby have something in it for us, today? Could it be some kind of map?" murmured Precious.

She yawned, and stretched, pulling her shoulders and elbows back. She raised her forearms and clenched her fists.

"I am so sleepy," she said.

Dreamer reached over and took her hand.

"Not far to the secret entrance to box canyon valley, a few more steps—we'll be safe for the night."

The moon had not risen past the mountains. It was a very dark night. Dreamer was feeling his way—one hand on the mountainside, one hand holding onto Precious.

The path turned right. They had not gone far when Dreamer touched the large metal ring that opened a door to a hidden tunnel. Dreamer tugged on the ring; a door swung open with the sound of grating metal, a creaking and a screech.

Precious did not want to go inside. It was dark, too dark to see what might be in store for her.

"There is a kind of bed inside that will take us to a safe canyon while we sleep," said Dreamer. "It is softer than sleeping on this rocky ground."

Dreamer helped Precious climb over something. It felt like a wall, to Precious. When she was over it and standing on the other side, she was standing on ground that was springy under her feet.

She heard Dreamer struggling with something.

"What is it?" she asked.

"Releasing, lifting the log—replacing it in a certain niche allows the ride."

As he said ride, he scrambled over the wall and lay down on the springy ground—really a mattress of twigs and branches. He pulled Precious down close beside him.

Fair Maiden

Precious snuggled her head into Dreamer's shoulder and said, "Tell me about your grandmother. Tell me Fair Maiden's story."

And so he began: Fair Maiden's father was ruler of a kingdom of rolling hills and beautiful farms and clear water brooks. He was king and he thought it was his duty to control everything in his kingdom. He dispensed justice and medicines and defended the kingdom and thought that that was the way to a happy life and a happy kingdom.

His daughter, Fair Maiden, was of a different mind and when she was among the people, administering the king's remedies, she also taught them where to find the healing herbs and how to use them for themselves. She pointed out to them, that there was wisdom inside a peaceful heart and that they could settle their own disputes.

One day she was by the brook, talking to some of the king's subjects about a new herb that one of them had found, when a handsome prince of a neighboring kingdom stopped by the brook that divided the kingdoms. He saw her on the other side of the brook and fell in love with her. She didn't even notice the prince but high on his castle hill, the king was watching. He noticed the prince gazing at his daughter. Suddenly there was heat in his neck, rising to his face. His face was red and his hands were shaking.

At first he thought he was angry that anyone, that a stranger would be staring at his daughter, but then he had a sinking feeling in his belly and he remembered the sinking feeling he had just before his beloved wife died—when he knew he had no remedy for her illness and when he knew he was going to lose her.

The king jumped on his mighty white stallion and galloped down into the valley; right into the middle of the peaceful gathering by the brook. He pulled hard on the reins and his horse reared up on two legs.

The people scattered as he reached down and scooped the princess up in his arms and put her on his horse and cantered home to the castle—all the while screaming at the princess, telling her she was in danger. Finally, the king dragged her down to a dark basement dungeon and locked her in it.

Big tears rolled down Fair Maiden's cheeks and she protested that she was not in any danger but still he would not release her. To comfort herself, Fair Maiden sang songs her mother sang to her so many years ago when she was a young child—before the plague claimed her mother's life.

The princess was not seen again. The king's subjects began to wonder what happened to her. They thought they heard her sad songs echoing as they gathered at the huge well just outside the castle but they didn't know what to make of it until—

One day a young page who lived at the castle was fetching water for the king and he told them that the princess was a prisoner in her own father's castle.

When the citizens of the kingdom heard that their princess was a prisoner, they were amazed and whispered among themselves about how she might be rescued. They remembered there was a prince in the kingdom across the brook who had amassed an army of faithful followers. After some discussion, they agreed that someone should contact this prince and seek his help to free their princess.

Brave One knocked on the door and he was greeted by a page who asked him, "What business do you have with our prince?"

When Brave One explained his mission, the page raised both hands and then clasped them together.

"The prince is already in love with your princess. He told me the moment he caught sight of her across the brook, his heart began to beat faster and faster and he knew he would marry her one day. He has been planning to come to your kingdom to ask the king for her hand in marriage."

When the prince heard the news that the king had imprisoned his own daughter, he changed his mind about asking the king for her hand in marriage.

He queried Brave One:

Tell me everything you know about the king and the princess. The more we know, the easier it will be to find a strategy to rescue the princess, to preserve both kingdoms and to save face for the king. There is no victory if any part of the kingdom is harmed. Victory only comes to those who know themselves and respect others.

The prince changed his clothes and donned the simple garb of the people so that he might slip across the brook without arousing suspicions of the king. Then he mounted his horse and rode with Brave One to a secret rescue-planning meeting. The prince looked each person there in the eye and said:

Even little things are important and we can't know which one may become a key to open the lock on a king's dungeon.

Meanwhile in her dark and dreary dungeon, the princess was noticing a barred opening that looked like it connected to a tunnel. A breeze blew in from the tunnel and she felt it brush against her face and lift a few strands of her blonde hair. She sensed that something good was about to happen.

She grabbed hold of the bars and put her face against them and took deep breaths of fresh air. Orange crumbly rust coated her hands. She looked at her hands and then grabbed the bars again. The bars squeaked, and wiggled. She could feel her heart pounding. She held her breath as she tried to remove one bar.

But then footsteps— She heard her father's footsteps approaching the dungeon. Quickly she stepped away from the bars and brushed the rust from her hands.

The king was carrying his golden lantern as he came down the dark hallway to the castle dungeons. He set the lantern down and just opened a small window in the door to Fair Maiden's prison.

"Come closer," he said, as he reached through the window to stroke her long silky golden hair.

Then he slid in a tray with some of her favorite foods. "I will not lose you. You are my good fortune and you are safe in this dungeon."

He locked the window again and ascended to his throne room. When he was gone the princess finished her meal in the dimming light of the dungeon and then she paced back and forth wondering how she might persuade her father to free her.

Meanwhile the prince was questioning each one in the community that surrounded the well, about what they knew. They reported that they heard Fair Maiden's voice as they were drawing water at the well and so that very same night, the prince and a large group of them gathered around the well. It was close to dusk when they heard Fair Maiden's sad song.

The prince whispered.

"It sounds like it is coming from the bottom of the well."

He put his finger to his lips and motioned for silence. When all were still and it was quiet, he bent down—leaned into the well and whispered.

"Fair Maiden."

She was startled to hear her name whispered to her. It seemed to be coming from the barred way. There was silence and then she could hear a muffle of other voices. She was afraid to make a sound.

The prince straightened up again.

"Is there someone, brave and strong enough to lower me down into that well?"

The same young man, who fetched him from his kingdom, stepped forward and took hold of the crank for lowering and bringing the bucket up.

The bucket for this well was huge—constructed of water proof wood strong enough to carry an enormous weight of water. The prince climbed into the bucket and was slowly lowered into the well as the others surrounded the well and stood guard to warn him, should anyone from the castle approach them.

When the bucket reached water level, the young man above, stopped unwinding the rope. He leaned over the well and whispered.

"Do you see anything?"

"A ledge," said the prince.

There was a ledge just above the water and it was wide enough for a person to stand on. He stepped out of the bucket and onto the ledge and began to walk around the inside of the well—all the time listening for the voice of the princess.

Just then the king's page came to the well and asked the people, "What are you doing here?"

A fast thinking spokesman said, "We come to the well to sing and give thanks for the cool clear water we draw from it."

The others around the well followed the spokesman's clue and began to make up a song as they held hands and danced around the well.

They sang out loud and clear.

"A page joins us in our celebration of cool refreshing water."

Alerted to the danger, the prince stopped walking and listened.

The page spoke softly but firmly to those gathered at the well.

"As soon as you have drawn water you must leave. The king sits at the window in his tower bedroom and he is disturbed that there are so many of you at the well—too many too close to the castle and especially at night."

The young man at the crank knew he would have to draw water or the page would begin to wonder what they were doing there. Unwinding the crank again he sang, "The bucket goes deeper into the well now. We shall have cool clear water to drink."

The prince heard the words of the song and he was glad that he was already out of the bucket and safely on the ledge. As the young man wound the heavy water- filled bucket back up, those gathered around began to sing again.

"We must leave you for a while deep well but we shall return for another bucket of water in the morning– as the king allows."

The prince was left on the ledge of the well with no way out but he heard what was being sung above. He knew he would be lifted up again.

Night clouded up over the well and it was so dark the prince just sat down on the ledge and listened to the sounds of the night. One owl called to another owl. There was a rustle of leaves in trees as a wind began to blow. Clouds parted for a few brief moments and revealed a part of the moon—a sliver of moon reflected in the water of the well.

His eyes were becoming accustomed to the dark and he could see the ledge going all the way around the inside of the well. He thought he saw a very dark spot on the wall across from where he was. He began to edge his way around to see if he could get closer to it.

If it gets too dark to see what it is, I might still touch it and know what it is.

As the prince was getting closer to the dark spot, he heard faint sounds. It sounded like sobbing.

Just then clouds covered the moon again and he was without its light. He sat back down on the ledge and waited. From time to time he splashed water on his face to keep from falling asleep.

Fair Maiden was quietly sobbing when she thought she heard the sound of water splashing. It sounded like it was coming from the barred way. She ran over to the bars and grabbed hold of them again. Twisting, pushing, pulling, she removed one bar and then another and another.

The prince heard the sound of metal rubbing against metal. He whispered.

"*Fair Maiden.*"

She stopped what she was doing and whispered, "*Who calls my name?*"

She was quiet, listening for a reply when she heard.

"*It is I, Justin Noble, prince of your neighboring kingdom and I have come to rescue you but I don't know where you are or how to find you.*"

Fair Maiden whispered again.

"*We must be close to one another. We can talk in whispers and still hear one another. Where are you?*"

"*Deep in a well. I am sitting on a ledge above the water.*"

He removed his sandals.

"*Listen, you can hear my feet splashing in the water.*"

Fair maiden was silent for a few moments and then she said, "*I am in my father's dungeon and there is a barred opening at the far end of this room. The bars are rusty and crumbling. I have already removed some of them.*"

They were both silent for a few moments. Then Justin remembered the dark spot on the wall.

Fair Maiden remembered feeling a breeze of fresh air. She remembered smelling fresh water when she put her face to the bars.

They both said it together—in one voice, "*There must be a tunnel that connects the dungeon to the well.*"

They were surprised to hear their own voices in unison, saying the same words, and it startled them into silence.

A breeze was stirring overhead and it moved the clouds again. Reflected light from half of the full moon lit the inside of the well. Fair Maiden saw a glimmering of light at the end of the tunnel.

Justin located the dark spot on the wall again. He put his sandals back on and quickly walked toward it. The closer he came to it the more it looked like a hole in the wall of the well.

As he was standing in front of it, he heard Fair Maiden say, "*Now, something is blocking the light at the end of this tunnel.*"

Justin heard an ominous noise. It was a page carrying a lantern with a squeaky handle. The page was coming to the well. His lantern was swinging in the breeze. He looked into the well. Quietly, Justin crawled into the tunnel and hid himself. He whispered to Fair Maiden.

"*Be still; a page comes to the well.*"

The page was there because the king woke from his dream about a well, with a full moon reflecting in the water.

As he pondered his dream, he remembered his subjects gathered at the well. The king's eyesight and hearing were not what they used to be and because he wanted a better understanding of what might have gone on at the well, he rang the bell for his young page.

And so it was that the page was leaning over the edge of the well, holding the king's lantern. He saw nothing in the well at first and then, when he thought he saw something in the water, he discovered it was his own reflection.

Fair Maiden and the prince didn't make a sound. A cricket chirped. Two owls called to one another.

The page looked up and back over his shoulder, just as the clouds parted and the light of the full moon allowed him to see one owl spread its wings and swoop down toward him. He held his lantern high in the air and the owl flew by him.

Back at the castle, he reported to the king.

"Owls are calling to their mates and one owl swooped down very close to me."

"What did you see in the well?" the king asked.

"The clouds had not parted yet, when I looked into the well and so I just saw reflections of myself and the lantern I was holding and I heard a cricket chirping."

"But, did you see a full moon?" the king asked.

"Yes, the full moon was revealed to me. I did see it."

Many times in the king's lifetime—whenever important changes were coming, he dreamed about the moon reflecting in water.

Just before he met the maiden, Fair, who was to become his bride and queen, he dreamed of seeing a sliver of moon reflecting in a brook. The reflection looked like the rim of a goblet to the king and he said to himself, "*I am going to taste fine wine.*"

Shortly before their princess, Fair Maiden, was born, the king dreamed of the moon again. It was reflecting in the common well of the kingdom. The moon was a little fuller than a sliver and it looked like a goblet tilted to one side. The king interpreted his dream.

My good fortune overflows and spills out into the kingdom.

One night before a virulent plague broke out in the kingdom, the king dreamed of a moonless night and in the dream he heard a warning voice and felt a cold wind that whispered: *Your family is in danger.*

It wasn't long after the dream that the queen fell ill and died of a disease that the king had no remedy for.

This night the king was remembering his previous dreams and what they meant to him. The full moon dream he had this night defied his interpretation and he was more than puzzled; he was disturbed by it.

He went back to his window and stared at the full moon darting in and out of clouds. No answer came to him. He grew weary and when the clouds completely covered the full moon again, he dismissed his page and went back to his sleep.

Breathing Together

fair Maiden and the prince were quiet for a long time—not even daring to whisper to one another. The moon seemed to move in and out of the clouds—riding ever higher across the sky. Finally a whole, bright full moon reflected in the water of the well.

Justin looked for other reflections in the water. He did not see any evidence that the page was still there. But he was silent and listened for danger from above. All he heard was the cheerful chirp of a cricket.

He was almost in a kind of sleepy reverie as he listened to the chirps. But then quite suddenly, he was more alert, He couldn't believe it. Was the cricket deliberately chirping each time he breathed in and chirping again as he breathed out?

Justin decided to test his observation to see if it were true. He inhaled more slowly counting:

One two three four—as he breathed in.

Then he held his breath counting:

One two three four—before he breathed out again.

One two three four five six—

He held his breath.

The cricket was pacing him, chirping with each in-breath and out-breath. Suddenly Justin knew it was true.

We are breathing together.

Justin received the feeling of calm and contentment the cricket was feeling and he fell back into a reverie and then he saw—almost as in a dream— a vision of a queen smiling at him.

He called out.

"Fair Maiden."

A sleepy princess was wakened.

"What? Be careful. Someone might hear you. You woke me. I was dreaming that I saw my mother. She was smiling at me."

Justin was silent—wondering.

The princess whispered.

"Did you hear me?"

He splashed his face with water.

"Yes! And I am astounded. In a kind of awake dream, I thought I saw a queen too and she was smiling at me."

He began to describe the queen to the princess. She interrupted him.

"It is my mother you are describing."

Justin began crawling down the long dark tunnel between them. Fair Maiden was humming an encouraging tune and trying to manipulate the bars at her end of the tunnel. She was able to remove one more bar.

When he reached the end of the tunnel, their hands touched through the open space she made. They held hands and whispered and whispered about how they might escape from the well. Eventually they closed their eyes and fell asleep.

Fair Maiden awakened the next morning when she heard her father's footsteps coming to the dungeon. She woke the prince and put her fingers to her lips.

He nodded his head and very quickly and quietly scooted further into the tunnel.

As quickly as she could, she was placing the bars she removed, back into place again.

The king called to her to come to the door of the dungeon but he didn't unlock the door. He just opened the window again and stroked her long blonde hair and left her breakfast tray. But then he hesitated.

Somehow the king sensed something was not the same.

She seems happier. What has changed? Does she know that I am right about the danger? Yes, finally she knows I am just protecting her. I can keep her safe forever inside this dungeon.

He shut the window again.

When the king's footsteps faded away the two of them worked on the bars and removed so many that Justin could crawl through the opening and into the dungeon with Fair Maiden. She shared her tray with him and then they sat side by side, holding hands, waiting—

Hours passed. Justin put his arm around Fair Maiden and she rested her head against his shoulder. There was no way to know when the people of the kingdom might return to the well with a plan to rescue them.

All through the night, people of the kingdom had conferred with one another about how they might deceive the king and still save the kingdom and when the plan was finally conceived, it took some time to put it in place.

It was because the princess had shared her knowledge with them and had encouraged them to use their own intelligence to find herbal remedies for themselves and to find answers to their own disputes all these years, that this new complicated task didn't seem much different to them.

A spokesman for the core group of rescuers summed up the strategy for the rest of the citizens:

Working together, using our talents (what each one can do best) we will not only rescue the prince and princess but we will save face for the king and preserve the kingdoms.

Early next morning, the Storyteller of the kingdom was sent to the castle to tell the king stories about magicians who traveled from kingdom to kingdom casting spells and performing amazing feats.

Storyteller told the king tales about one master magician's powers and how he could cast spells on anyone. The spelled-out person would then obey, the magician—or whoever had purchased the spell from the magician.

The Storyteller leaned closer to the king and whispered to emphasize.

"It may be possible for you to purchase such a spell because this magician has just arrived from the far ends of the earth. He is visiting our kingdom, this very day."

As Storyteller was leaving the castle, the son of Observer in the kingdom ran into the throne room. In an out-of-breath voice he reported to the king.

"There is an illness in the valley. We need the king's herbal remedies. Please let the princess bring them to us."

The king didn't even consider releasing her. He dismissed Observer's son.

"I will bring remedies to the kingdom, myself."

And so early that morning he was gathering a little of each royal herb in his gardens—bending over and straightening up so many times that he had a painful kink in his back.

He was beginning to realize that getting on his horse and riding to the valley would not be a pleasant journey and would not be good for his aching back and so he stopped to ponder what he might do. Storyteller's tale came to his mind.

If the princess were under a magical spell and had to obey me, I could release her from the dungeon. She could carry my remedies to the kingdom again. I must purchase this magical spell from the magician.

The king rang a bell for his page.

Meanwhile some of the citizens of the kingdom who were skilled woodworkers had been working all through the night and into the morning, creating a life-size puppet of the princess. One carver created a foot, another carver created a hand, another a leg, another an arm.

The woodworkers worked quickly and surely and they were so skilled at working with one another and checking and cross checking with one another to make sure the body of work and all the parts fit together, that when it was done, even they were surprised at how perfectly it fit together and how beautiful it was—their life-sized doll.

Just to make sure it would fool the king, Observer was called to look at the puppet.

He said, "Indeed, you have made a very good replica of the princess but it must have hair—the real hair of the princess, glued onto its head because I have noticed whenever the king greets the princess, he strokes her hair."

Another conference was quickly called together. A Scribe wrote instructions on a piece of scroll. The daughter of a Woodworker volunteered to sing at the well to attract the prince's attention.

She pushed the scroll up her sleeve and she and a strong young man went to the well to lower the bucket.

Justin heard the crank unwinding but he didn't know who was at the well.

The daughter of the Woodworker slipped the piece of scroll into the bucket as it was being lowered into the well and she began to sing.

"Drawing water from the well, one never knows what magic might unfold from a bucket."

Justin whispered to Fair maiden.

" A *strange song! I must look into that bucket before it hits the water."*

He scooted down the tunnel, stepped onto the ledge and reached for the bucket. The scroll rolled out but he grabbed it before it fell into the water. On the outside of the scroll, it said in big letters—RESCUE PLANS.

An empty bucket was cranked up to those above as the prince crawled down the tunnel again.

As he squeezed through the rusty opening and back into the dungeon, the princess asked, "What is that you have in your hand?"

She took the scroll from him and read it and when she knew the steps they would have to take, tears came to her eyes.

As soon as Justin was standing on his two feet again he took her in his arms and comforted her and then he read the scroll.

The princess had never cut her long blonde beautiful hair and she didn't want to part with it but (according to the scroll) for the rescue plan to work, she must somehow cut her hair and then get it to the woodcarvers.

The prince said, "I don't know why they didn't put some scissors in the bucket with the scroll."

They didn't have long to wonder about what the princess might use to cut her hair. The prince put his finger to his lips and whispered.

"Footsteps."

Fair Maiden nodded, yes, as Justin scurried back into the tunnel. She was re-placing rusty bars just as the king was opening the window to her dungeon.

He called the princess to him and stroked her golden hair once again and then he instructed her.

"You must cut a piece of cloth from the hem of your dress—as long and as wide as your little finger. I will measure it to make sure you have done it correctly. I have a delicious surprise for you when it is done."

The king handed her a pair of scissors. The princess was puzzled by his request and she was surprised to find in her hands—*the very tool I need to cut my hair.*

She cut a piece of cloth from the hem of her dress. The king was so busy measuring the cloth and her little finger that he didn't remember the shears and she shoved them into a dark corner of the dungeon.

As he slid a beautiful tray of food in through the dungeon window, the king said, "Perhaps you will sit on the throne beside me this evening."

Then he stroked her hair and shut the window. Her hand went to her forehead and her eyes dropped to the floor.

The plan—the plans say the bucket will be lowered again at midnight.

She was quiet, listening. When she could no longer hear his footsteps, she whispered.

"How are we going to let the woodcarvers know that we might need to leave before midnight?"

The prince had no answers but the cricket was in the well again and heard her question. The cricket sang and offered to help.

It paced its chirps to correspond to the breathing pattern of the prince again. It chirped a few words as he breathed in and it chirped a few words as he breathed out. They reached a kind of rapport and a magical connection was made between them.

Because the prince was unperturbed and quiet and contemplating the answer to Fair Maiden's question, he heard the cricket chirp:

When the princess cuts her hair, I will carry one strand to the top of the well and to Observer. When Observer sees it he will know.

Excitedly, Justin whispered.

"It can be done. Listen! Even a cricket is helping us. It will carry one strand of your hair to the top of the well."

Fair Maiden shook her head.

A cricket talks to him. Please don't let it be a dream.

As she retrieved the shears from their dark corner, tears trickled down her cheeks. A lock of hair was in her hand. The first cut was agony but after that it was quickly done. She gave one strand of golden hair to the prince.

He crawled down the tunnel and gave it to the now silent cricket—clinging to a rock on the inside of the well.

The cricket struggled with the golden strand. It was difficult carrying it around large rocks that were jutting out of the side of the well.

Justin could hear Fair Maiden sobbing.

Worries began to plague him.

Would Observer notice a small cricket underfoot? Could a cricket even find Observer? Maybe the cricket would be stepped on before it could deliver its golden strand.

There were quite a few courses of rocks to climb and the cricket was really struggling with its load. It was stopping and dropping the golden strand on one rock after another.

Justin was watching its progress.

The cricket rested and sang a few notes at the half-way mark before it picked up its burden again but then it couldn't go on. Something was stopping it.

The golden strand was caught in a crack. The cricket had to back up and nearly fell in the well trying to free its gold.

Justin scooted back into the tunnel. Someone was peering into the well.

It was the son of Observer who had come to the well. He saw the cricket holding onto a strand of golden hair.

Observer had been teaching his son to be an Observer too and so the son was noticing everything about that cricket.

That cricket is not singing—and crickets sing. That cricket is carrying a heavy golden strand of hair—and crickets do not hold onto heavy burdens.

As the son ran home to tell his father what he had observed, the cricket was making one last valiant effort to carry gold to the top of the well. It was more than the cricket could manage.

The golden strand of hair fell back into the water and floated by the prince. Justin didn't see the quick, knowing glance of Observer's son. He was disappointed that his plan had not worked out as he had imagined it would.

His fears spoke to Fair Maiden,

"We may be stuck here—forever, prisoners of your father. The golden strand we gave to the cricket floats in the water now. We have to do something. Perhaps when your father comes to the dungeon I can over-power him."

Fair Maiden shook her head, no.

"No, we mustn't use force. My father has been a good man, and a kind king. It frightens him that he might lose me. He has been so sad that he was not able to save my mother from the plague. He misses her."

"It affects his judgment. That's why he acts the way he does now. We must find another way. He deserves our respect and every effort we can make to save his face."

"The people of the kingdom have come up with a good plan. I know it. There may be some set-backs along the way but it will all work out. When we do escape this dungeon, we must not just run away. We will never be free if we have to fear the pursuit of my father's armies."

The cricket was singing a happy cricket song again. It knew Observer's son saw the heavy burden it was carrying. It knew Observer would get the message and so it sang.

Observer will know and then you can go. Everything will be all right.

Justin was feeling rebuffed and a little grumpy and not in the mood for listening to a cricket that had failed to carry its burden to the top of the well.

The cricket was too happy to breathe in rhythm with a grumpy prince and so the distracted Justin did not hear the cricket's good news.

Fair Maiden shook her head and smiled at the discouraged prince, thinking:

I love to hear a cricket sing. It reminds me of my mother's songs, my mother's stories, the things she taught me when I was only a little girl.

I remember my mother telling me that some misfortunes are really not misfortunes but necessary delays or lessons on the way to something much better in a lifetime. She said we are surprised and rewarded for our patience and persistence in going through tough times.

Justin was silent.

Suddenly Fair Maiden's eyes widened and her mouth fell open and she almost shouted.

"I must put my dress in the bucket too. The Seamstresses of the kingdom may have made a dress for the dummy, just like mine, but it won't have a cut in the hem to match the piece my father has."

Tears came to her eyes as she shook her head and reached up and brushed back her now very short golden tresses.

The prince put one arm around her shoulder and the other under her chin. He was tilting her face up and looking into her eyes.

"You are beautiful even when you are crying."

While they were waiting in the dungeon, the king was busy completing tasks the magician had given him.

I must accomplish them before he will supply the magical spell.

The king was tiring and talking to himself.

I fetched a goblet of water from the brook, a piece of cloth from the hem of her dress—the exact same size as her little finger. I counted every step from this bedchamber to the doorway of the dungeon.

I must add one for every window on the way—subtract one for every key on my key ring.

Remember—I must remember—must carry that number in my head and then tell the number to no one but the magician.

The king did not want to make a mistake because he really loved his daughter and he didn't want any harm to come to her because of what he did or didn't do. He trembled remembering the magician's warnings.

If you speak that magical number before your tasks are completed, the spell will become unstable and the consequences are not predictable.

If you make one mistake in your measurements, your daughter will be in grave danger. She may become a doll—instead of a daughter who will obey your every command.

It had taken the king all day and into early evening to complete his tasks. His feet were dragging. To the brook and back, fetching water for the magician had been a long walk. He was exhausted.

As he delivered the evening tray of food to Fair Maiden he was still concentrating on his counting and he just mumbled to her.

"Maybe tomorrow, you will sit on the throne."

Justin and Fair Maiden sighed a sigh of relief and cat-napped and waited for midnight.

The king retired to his bedchamber early that night and he dreamed again about the full moon reflecting in well water.

At midnight, when all was quiet on the castle grounds, the bucket was lowered into the well. The sound of the crank woke Justin and he nudged Fair Maiden. They crawled down the tunnel and stood on the ledge. As she was undressing, she whispered.

"Be careful!"

When the bottom of the bucket touched the surface of the water, Justin reached for it.

Fair Maiden barely had time to drop her hair into it when the cranking began again and she had to toss her dress at the bucket. It was hanging over the edge of the bucket as it ascended.

The one who lowered the bucket was surprised to see Fair Maiden's dress draped there. Then he saw the piece cut out of the hem and it donned on him.

He nodded yes, and whispered into the well.

"It takes everyone working together to have a successful plan."

The woodworkers glued one strand of hair after another onto the doll's head. Finally, Observer stroked the doll's head and was satisfied. It was dressed and placed in the bucket and then lowered into the well and into the waiting arms of Justin and the princess.

It took both of them to lift the doll out of the bucket and drag it down the tunnel. When they set it in the dungeon they were surprised at how life-like a doll could be.

It had been a long day and night of waiting and not long after they put their burden down, Justin and Fair Maiden fell asleep in one another's arms.

Next morning, when the king woke, he called for the magician and whispered the magic number to him.

"NOW Give Me The Spell I Asked For," he shouted.

The magician spoke softly, calmly.

"The potion is ready. Ingredients have been mixed in this goblet. When you sprinkle the potion on your daughter's head she will appear to become wooden but she will obey your every command. Are you sure you have measured everything correctly?"

He emphasized again.

"You Must Have Measured Everything Correctly."

He waved his hand back and forth in front of the kings eyes as if asking him to wake up— to take some time to reconsider his scheme. The king just nodded his head, yes.

Now, the magician was standing face to face with him, speaking very quietly. *"You can still change your mind. Do you want to chance having a daughter who may not be able to think for herself again?"*

The king didn't think that was so bad.

After all, he told himself, *who better to think for her, than me?*

And so it was that he said, "Get on with it. I will cast the spell."

As the king was paying the magician for his spell, Observer's son approached the king and repeated his request.

"Please send the princess into the kingdom with her remedies."

The magician whispered in the king's ear.

"Rest assured that if your calculations have not been correct, the rest of the kingdom need not know it. Even if the princess turns to wood, the rest of the kingdom will see her as she always was, as long as you keep her by your side and carry her everywhere you go."

The king nodded at Observer's son.

"Your wish will soon be granted."

He didn't even take a moment to ponder—to consider the magician's whispers. He rushed down stairs to the dungeon, to sprinkle the potion on his daughter's head. He called to her as he approached the door.

"I have something for you—something to show you."

Justin scrambled into the tunnel. Fair Maiden didn't have time to re-position the bars. The king was opening the window looking for her—for her golden hair so that he could sprinkle the potion on her head.

She was crouched behind the doll, holding it upright next to the window in the dungeon door.

The king was concentrating on his daughter's hair and was not noticing anything else. He almost reached out to stroke it but he was afraid she might move away before he could sprinkle the potion.

I will sprinkle the potion and then I will open the door and stroke her hair.

He reached through the window and sprinkled the potion on the doll's head. Then he searched for his key. He fumbled with it, dropped it and finally opened the door and reclaimed a wooden daughter.

Justin and Fair Maiden were crawling down the tunnel and heading for the well where the bucket was already lowered and waiting for them. As they stepped into the bucket, there was a loud creak—a protesting creak. It was straining under their combined weight.

The strength of the arm of the young man, who was turning the crank, was severely tested. Even using both arms he was having trouble lifting the two of them to the rim of the well. He called for help, but there was no one near enough to hear him, except the cricket.

It hopped and jumped as fast as it could to the home of Observer. Observer's son was there and so it sailed onto his shoulder and began to sing in rhythm with the boy's breathing. It wasn't long before the boy understood what the cricket was singing about. He ran to his father and told him what he heard and how he heard it.

Observer was amazed at what his son was telling him.

"If this is true, you have discovered something new and you are not only an Observer but a Listener too. We will go to the well together and see if the strongest young man in our kingdom needs our help."

When Observer and his son reached the well, the crank was not moving. Justin and Fair Maiden were not close enough to the rim of the well to take hold and pull themselves out. There was a strained look on the young man's face. His muscles were bulging and he was sweating.

"Quickly, we must put our hands to the crank, before he loses his grip," Observer whispered.

They all pushed and pulled together. The crank began to move— to turn again. Finally the bucket was raised high enough for the two escapees to reach the rim but they were only standing beside the well for a few moments when a page from the castle approached them.

No one spoke. They all held their breath. The page motioned for them to move away from the well and he quickly took hold of the crank.

He didn't recognize the prince or the princess in her tunic like undergarment and short hair. She looked just like another page to him .

"I will draw water before you do. I am drawing water for the princess. The king has finally released her from his dungeon."

As the king opened the dungeon door he heard a thud and caught his breath and then muttered to himself.

"What have I done? Is she wooden? Have I miscalculated?"

He stroked the hair of the doll lying on the floor. He picked it up and carried it to the throne room and then he sat it beside him. While he was resting from his efforts, he looked at the doll again and again.

Finally, though there was no one to hear him, he voiced his doubts.

"Surely this is a doll and a sly trick of that magician."

But it wasn't long before he noticed the hem of the doll's dress. Confusing, hopeful thoughts ran around in his head.

No, it has to be the princess. She is still just a little wooden from the spell. She will recover when I order a new dress for her.

He called to his page.

"Go to the dressmakers. The princess must have a new dress. She wears absolutely perfect royal clothes—no tears in the hem. Be sure it is a gown just like the one she is wearing."

It was then that he called a second page to go to the well and fetch water for the princess and he called for a third page to fetch the magician.

When the magician—who was really a very ordinary citizen of the kingdom— arrived at the throne, he whispered in the king's ear.

"Only you will know. I know it troubles you that the daughter who sits forever willingly beside you has become a wooden puppet. No one needs to know you have traded one fear for another."

" It is too late. The spell cannot be undone, but for a small sum I can give you words that will quell the questions your subjects may have about your daughter."

The king was silent for a few moments and then he nodded his head and paid the magician a few more pieces of gold.

The magician clapped his hands twice.

"I know a newlywed royal couple who live in an adjoining kingdom. The young princess looks much like your daughter but she has very short blonde hair. I will cast a spell to persuade her to carry your remedies into the kingdom and to take care of you in your old age."

The king was tired and wise enough this time to listen, really listen to the magician and he nodded his head, yes.

"But, he pleaded, is there no way to undo the spell I cast on my daughter?"

The magician shook his head and shuffled one foot and threw his hands up and spoke so quietly no one else heard.

"I warned you. Now, listen! To save your face you must tell this story word for word, when anyone asks you about why you imprisoned your own daughter."

The magician told the king to say:

I kept the princess in my dungeon because she was under an evil sorcerer's spell. The sorcerer said if she left the castle she would sicken and die. I imprisoned her to keep her well until I could find a master magician to undo the spell.

When the master magician was found, I offered to pay him any sum he might ask for, if he would undo the sorcerer's spell. Unfortunately even he could not undo the whole spell but he was able to limit it.

The changes he made to the sorcerer's spell are these: As long as the princess is on the throne in the castle, she will be the same princess the kingdom has always known. Her hair will be long and blonde and silky.

When the princess leaves the castle, her life will not be shortened but her hair will be shorter instead.

Precious lifted her head and looked into Dreamer's eyes. "Why did the magician tell him to tell such a tale? Everyone knew."

Dreamer took her hand.

"It was for the king's benefit. The more he told the story, the more he came to believe it himself and eventually he accepted the doll and his daughter as herself."

Precious lifted her head again and looked around but it was too dark to see anything. She yawned and closed her eyes. She thought she could feel the bed they were lying on moving. There was a clickity, click clack—metallic sound as the bed moved.

"What is that sound?"

"Hard to explain; see when we wake," said Dreamer.

It was their lullaby as they fell asleep in one another's arms.

The Sharpie

A monstrous black bird was reflecting blue, green and purple from its feathers as it stretched out huge talons and prepared to land on the ledge jutting out from the mountain at the mouth of its cave. The tired bird was daydreaming.

Strands of gold against the mountainside—

Suddenly the earth trembled and the bird was jolted out of its reverie just as it touched the rock ledge.

"SSCEEEEIIMMMM"

Its fearful shriek echoed in the cave.

No, no! Not that nightmare again. Can a nightmare be following me—finding me here? No, my perch is intact. I am powerful and secure. No need to ruffle my feathers.

The earth shuddered again. Kicked up some dust in the bird's cave.

Not again—crumbling, earth rumbling— NO! Stop! I don't want to remember the running away, the stumbling! Mirror— why did I smash it? Terror— what didn't I want to see? Falling, skinning my knee while roads, sidewalks, brick buildings buckle—my clenched fist, white knuckles gone! How can it be?

The bird ruffled its feathers.

No, it's not then. I'm not there again. I'm here. I'm invincible. Safe in my cave. It's the earth that is trembling. I'm not resembling that someone running away. I'm in control and powerful—a powerful bird.

I'll understand his crack. I'll find my way back. What's in a name, in a word? Was he playing some kind of cruel game? Why did he tell me to remember my name?

As the Sharpie folded huge, black wings, strange shriek-whistles came out of its mouth. It looked over its shoulder at its wings.

*Not feathers—**feathers**— **claws**— no, **no**, what happened to me— to my hands and feet?*

The bird was shaking its head and pacing in its cave.

How did I escape—inside a metal fish, a metal bird? No, I'm losing it. Can't remember. Not the right word. Something ubiquitous—the square eye I'll look into it. I'll find him. Secrets are iniquitous!

The Sharpie screeched and stopped to look around the cave as if to find a square eye watching her there.

It is my birth-right, in the Land of Plenty— more, MORE. We all want more and I'll have mine when I find him.

She was lifting one foot, flexing her talons.

Birth pangs! That's what everyone said it was. But there were volcanic eruptions, severe weather, energy crises, earth quakes, mud slides, raging floods. And there was so much violence, killing and blood.

She was screeching. She lifted her wings and hopped and ruffled her feathers. She cocked her head. She was wandering aimlessly around in circles in her cave on the mountainside.

"*Is the nightmare here or there? Should I care?*"

She stomped her feet.

Why did he say, I fear, what you've broken can't be fixed, here? Eeeeeiii. Where does he go? Someone must know?

She sat back down; leaned on her tail— almost fell over backwards. She had to flap her wings to regain her balance, to keep from tipping over sideways.

Escape—Yes, I did escape. No thanks to him.

The bird began pacing back and forth, back and forth at the entrance to her cave.

How did he— was it at the university, he found the key? Halbert Onemug and his grand theory! I thought he said that it couldn't be true—leaping into other dimensions.

The bird stopped pacing—just stared at the morning sunlight streaming into the cave.

A bitter taste in my mouth—what is it I'm remembering? Oh, yes, he said there were only a few drops but I could see more than a few drops in the bottle— more than enough for both of us. He couldn't keep it from me.

She stomped her foot, blinked her eyes and cocked her head. She was hearing muffled sounds.

Sounds like shuffled footsteps, coming from somewhere above.

She scratched the claws of her right foot against a rough protruding rock in a side wall of the cave as if she were sharpening them. She was remembering his finger pointed at her. He was shaking it back and forth.

You don't know what you are doing. Don't ask me to pull strings for you. It would be like breaking the strings of a cocoon—the butterfly set free too soon.

Not allowed to struggle, not allowed to pump up its own wing muscles, a butterfly might be grounded forever—doomed to die before it glides on warm breezes, before it visits beautiful fragrant flowers. Little caterpillar, wait! One day you will be a butterfly and fly.

"I didn't wait and he was wrong. I ought to know. My wings carry me where I want to go. Two can play his game. He was just keeping secrets from me and his excuse was lame."

The bird lifted one foot up to her face as if she were inspecting her claw. She put that foot down and scratched with the other foot on her sharpening rock.

*Onemug's secrets and no more distress!—I will have them. I will be wise, certified, **a super sorceress**!*

The bird let out another ferocious,

"SSCEEEIIIM."

She looked at newly sharpened claws—contemplating again.

He didn't know I was watching him unroll those ancient manuscripts. Sufi tales, teaching stories, that's what he said they were. I peeked at some. They seemed ludicrous to me. Was he, were they hiding something in plain sight? He would laugh and then just sit there holding a scroll in his hand—sometimes for quite a while before he rolled it up again.

That bottle of bitter liquid was always beside him while he read those mysterious manuscripts. Was there some kind of transmission of secrets in the silence? I knew. We all knew that he had discovered something—something even he was in awe of.

The day he disappeared for a whole day—that same day I found his uncorked bottle. There were just a few sips left in it. When he reappeared he wouldn't say where he had been. Did he think he could hide his secrets from me? No, nooooo..... my foot!

There was an angry, grumbling growl growing in the back of the Sharpie's throat.

The last thing I remember—bottle in my hand. Something was inscribed on the cork: Q- u- a- n- t- Y- n- n- a- l- i- n- e. What harm could there be in just a few drops?

He has no right to keep it from me. I shouldn't have to steal a sweet taste of it. Oh, no—it was bitter! I remember bitter. Why, why wasn't it sweet?

She was pacing faster and faster, stomping and ruffling her wings. Finally, she flew up in the air and attacked the side wall of her own cave with outstretched claws. Again and again she attacked until the built up energy of her anger was drained. And then it came back to her.

She remembered the notations she read in Onemug's log.

Uncorked mysterious bottle. Tasted one drop on the tip of my tongue. Couldn't rescind. Mushroom explosion, whirl wind—another drop and I climbed onto a beam of light. Everything bright, couldn't stop, crunched heavier— closed my eyes. Breathing difficult—Forced to realize holding my breath is not wise. Heart pounding, time slowing— didn't know where I was going.

The bird held her breath, looked around.

I know where he went. He is here. Onemug, is the Wizard. He is here.

She began pacing around in ever smaller circles. In a kind of trance.

Numbers on a blackboard, tables in that room. Students taking notes, beakers and tubing—Onemug was pacing, speaking to the class.

She closed her eyes. She could almost hear his voice again.

Why did you do it? What will become of you? You will have to endure anxious feelings. You won't recognize yourself. There might be a kind of psychological reeling. I don't know how long the transformation might last.

It's not meant for anyone else. Take deep breaths, when everything seems to be going too fast. But don't close your eyes to what's going on around you.

I still don't know enough. I was just experimenting on myself. Rescuing you may be extraordinarily tough. If you only knew—

When she opened her eyes. There was a strange after taste in her mouth. Her heart was racing. She was holding her breath. She remembered hearing—

Breathe, breathe—you drank too much.

She took a deep breath and shook her head and blinked her eyes and let out a big-bird sigh.

Something, brought tears to his eyes and it was bitter, bitter, the last dregs of the bottle. That awful taste still on my tongue. My body felt different and strange, stiff and wider, heavier and lighter. He was running away from me. Something confused me. Is that how he eluded me?

I started running after him and I don't know how or why but I knew that I was about to fly. What did I see? I looked at the sky. It seemed to be beckoning me. I knew no impossibility. How high might I go? I had to know.

Impossible to leap from a cliff and survive some might say and yet, now I can glide. There's nowhere for him to hide. Ha, ha isn't it a shame? I was soaring over his head, higher and higher.

When I lift my wings on gusty up-draft wind current days, I can almost forget that I ever had feet and legs and that I tasted the dregs.

Carol C. McFall

But now that I'm a high flyer, I'm in a daze— not remembering, my thinking a haze. What was it I wanted—riches, fame? What was it he said? Remember my name?

Professor Halbert Onemug

Onemug looked out a physics classroom window at familiar star patterns. He knew it would soon be daylight. Hours had gone by but it seemed to be only a few minutes he spent here, or there, or somewhere. He was so disoriented he had no way of knowing what day it was. He glanced down the walkway, looking for a familiar sight. It was there—

Ginkgo trees standing majestically beside the brick walkway to Chapman Hall, the university building that housed science classrooms.

He was in deep thought, trying to reconstruct the past few days in his mind.

Saw her there, on that walkway—brilliant student, the beautiful young lady, following me like my shadow, never far away. Escape to my office. Step into solitude there. Oh, no—footsteps, her footsteps in the hallway and a knocking on my closed door.

Shari had been pestering him for days.

Your wife worried when you didn't go home for your evening meal. You were not in your lab. No one saw you leave. You are encouraging gossip.

She was wheedling, waiting for an explanation about his disappearances. He just smiled at her. He knew rumors were beginning to circulate about his disappearances. When he reappeared in his laboratory, he refused to give any explanation about where he had been.

Onemug discussed his work with only a few trusted colleagues and with an occasional brilliant student he thought had come to him for wisdom and not for secrets.

Even the magical square eye could not reveal his mysterious secret until—

The messenger, an elderly woman robed in a loose and flowing gown—

There was a look of astonishment on Onemug's face as he remembered her strange story.

We have been chanting: Quantym tym, tym, quantym tym, tym—for one day and one night. During the chanting, one elder of our ancient healing circle traveled to another dimension. (Though she appeared to be with us the whole time.) It was her intention to bring back a few drops of an ancient healing potion, she found— where someone, an old priest, maybe a caretaker in a patched robe was standing beside a four headed beast mumbling, whispering to himself, *"Onemug, my name is Onemug in another dimension."* We searched until we found you, here.

The story and her message had been very disturbing to Onemug. He closed his eyes, placed his elbows on his desk and loosely grasped his face with both hands—fingers to his forehead and thumbs to his cheeks. He was silent and waiting for some kind of enlightenment when he remembered.

It is coming back to me, the image of a four headed beast.

The elderly woman, the messenger, enjoyed silence and waited with him. When Onemug opened his eyes, she reached into the folds of her robe and brought out the bottle of precious liquid she was carrying. She said that one of their circle had been healed by a few drops of the medicine. The bottle was very much like the first almost empty bottle Onemug had discovered buried among some old manuscripts in a forgotten corner of the university library. Questions flooded into his mind.

Could someone else have the formula? Could someone else be testing it How? When? I have only just begun to work with it myself? I have not even discussed it with anyone.

Is there another way to get to where I have been? Does that other dimension, penetrate here and now at some unknown vortexes?

Could it be just some kind of coincidence that such disparate disciplines discover Ynnaline at almost the same instance?

Is it evidence of some higher purpose unfolding? Is that what the woman is suggesting to me?

She was almost out the door when she stopped and turned around to face him again. She had a strange look on her face and her voice was different. It had taken on a much deeper tone. Her whole body took on a different posture. The words that came out of her mouth were even stranger.

From deeper than a black hole we have walked a Maxi plank and leapt to be purposeful indeterminacy.

We used to be inexplicable quirks in your lingo—Colorful, Charming, Strange. We are a family so diverse we span more than one uni-verse. Names like gluons don't begin to describe us.

We are relatives but cannot be found anywhere at any one time. We are not confined by force-fields. We've escaped Edenic boundaries.

We're riding a kind of flood in a knower's arc, to where we're at, on top of the mountain of possibilities and inside the parallels of creative image-a-nation.

In no-time we create everything from nothing. What could be more fun for heavenly clowns? We tease about nothing that matters and we just can't stand still for Bohring physicists.

Ha ha and aha are not so far apart. Signing on and off for now. We are yours truly—a Quark

She left without another word. The message was so shocking, it stuck in his mind.

He was muttering, whispering to himself.

"Strange, very strange indeed! It can't be; can it? Priest? Caretaker? Quark?"

Onemug left his office and walked a well worn path of the university campus trying to remember what it was that he had been doing before that visitation.

Oh yes— there she is again, that student. Shari is still shadowing me.

Shari walked right up to him and began pleading.

"Teach me what you know about other dimensions and the Quantym message."

Onemug's thoughts were beginning to clear.

She must have overheard what the messenger was telling me.

He remembered thinking, if she overheard maybe she is meant to know but then he heard his own warning inner voice shouting, "No, NO." What could he say to discourage her?

"Do you hear that voice? Do you pay attention to your own inner voice? Mine says there are some fake students in this world."

She shook her head.

He cupped one hand around her ear..

"Be still and listen! "

He heard a strange bird-like shrieking, whistle ringing in his ear. Shari said she didn't hear anything.

It was all coming back to him. The last time he saw her she was shaking her head, questioning him.

You are confusing me. Why won't you answer my questions?"

The campus was almost back to normal—cleaned up after the earthquakes. But Shari had disappeared from campus, had not returned to her classes. No one had seen her.

He didn't want to believe it. Reluctantly he put two and two together and came up with five. He knew she was there in the valley. He would have to find a way to rescue her.

The Talking Horse

Precious and Dreamer woke to a warm, bright morning—sun shining down on them in their traveling bed.

"Where are we?" asked Precious.

"We are at the other end of the tunnel and we are about to enter the box canyon."

Words tumbled out of Precious, all in one breath, "How did we get here? What kind of magic bed is this? Let's go find a horse of a different color."

Dreamer drawled, "Not so fast. Slow down. This is as far as the bed takes us. Climb out of the bed."

He pointed.

"There's a safe haven canyon ahead of us. We'll find Talking Horse. The horses may know valley secrets, I don't know, yet. It was Talking Horse who showed me the magic bed and the path of metal it rides on."

"Honorable wheels allow the bed to move back and forth on its path to the box canyon. The horse can pull it back up to the door along the inside mountain path we took."

Precious crawled over the side of the bed, jumped down onto the ground, touched the metal path and said, "The track is cold."

Dreamer just shook his head.

"Sunshine warms it up, Come on. We must find something to eat."

Dreamer was struggling with something.

"What are you doing?" asked Precious.

"I am setting the log. Talking horse calls it a brake— to hold the bed here."

Precious didn't understand what he was talking about but she didn't really want to know any more about it.

Magic! It really must be magic. We traveled in a magic bed.

"There are some fruit and nut trees not too far from here," said Dreamer.

He angled off to the right of the tunnel. They were walking on soft lush grasslands and Precious heard the twittering of birds as they approached the beginning of a forest of fruit and nut trees.

Trees seemed to bow down to them as they passed by. Were they offering the fruits of their branches to Precious and Dreamer?

Precious tasted one.

"They taste like the dried fruits of the desert—chewy and sweet."

After they had eaten their fill, Dreamer puckered his lips. He put his pointing finger and his little finger in his mouth. He pushed the two fingers together with his thumb and laid them on his tongue and closed his lips around his fingers. Then he blew on them. Out came a loud whistle.

Precious giggled.

"How? What noise did you make?"

"I am calling Talking Horse."

Dreamer continued whistling and whistling as they walked. They were getting deeper and deeper into the wooded area around box canyon. Finally he stopped.

"I can't believe it—no Talking Horse and no other horses in sight either. I wonder where the horses have gone? The mothers and foals stay here for the foal's first year according to Talking Horse."

Precious and Dreamer came out of the trees into a clearing and caught a glimpse of a foal following its mother to the far end of the canyon.

Galloping toward them, head held high, nostrils flared and tail swishing, was Talking Horse. He kicked up a cloud of dust as he approached them on the path the horses made in the canyon.

Talking Horse stopped abruptly, in front of Precious.

"You frightened the mothers and they are running away with their colts."

"Precious won't harm them," said Dreamer. "The horses accept me; what is so different about, Precious?"

"Horses do not trust princesses," said the horse. "It has to do with gathered horse lore. Some stories have become sacred horsestories. The story about a princess who couldn't keep a secret may be what has spooked them."

"What story is that?" asked Precious.

"I can't believe you don't know the story?"

Dreamer told her about the ancient tale. That the princess was married to a prince who was enchanted as a horse. A wicked wizard put a spell on the prince so that his most valuable and magical powers were only available to him in his horse form. When he took human form he lost his powers and his magic.

The horse-prince in human form, married the princess but he was not able to keep his horse self a secret from her and he was not able to tell her the awful consequences if she told anyone else about his transformations. Every time he tried to tell her his story, he was transformed into a horse and she could not understand him. He did ask her to keep his secret, and she agreed to do it not knowing the whole story.

The princess loved the prince-horse very much and she was proud of his accomplishments. He was a valiant fighter and defeated many enemies of their kingdom and he provided her with everything she could wish for until—

One day her sisters came to visit her and they were bragging about their husband's riches and power and fine qualities. The princess was bursting to tell them about her husband's magical powers and transformations.

After all, she thought, what harm could there be in telling just my sisters, just my very own family?

She thrust her chest out and said in a loud voice, *"My husband is sometimes a horse—a magical horse."*

Her sisters laughed at her and no sooner had she said, *horse,* than her husband appeared at the door to their house. He was staggering. He had tears in his eyes.

Day by day he grew weaker and older and finally one day he confronted her.

"You told my secret; didn't you?"

"Yes, but if I had known what it would do to you, I surely wouldn't have done it Is there no remedy? I can't bear to see you suffering and growing old before my eyes."

His voice grew weaker and weaker.

"If I were to stay here, now, I would die in a few days. The only remedy is to leave you. I must dwell as a horse in the valley of horses. I can survive there— where a kindly old wizard dwells in a cave. Perhaps with his help, one day, we'll meet again."

The princess wept.

"Go! Be your magical horse self again in the land of horses."

The very next day everyone wondered but no one asked what happened to the prince. The princess never mentioned his name again—though she dreamed of him every night.

"I dream of her every night," said Talking Horse.

Dreamer shook his head.

" This sacred foaling ground must not be revealed prematurely but surely it may be found, at the right time—by a worthy seeker."

"I hope you are right, said Talking Horse, at this very moment, mothers and colts are gathering into a circle of wisdom to decide together what can be done to seal the lips of your princess."

Dreamer spoke to Talking Horse.

"Fresh and clear discernment of many colts added to the collective wisdom of their elders can solve almost any problem."

Talking Horse planted his feet with determination.

" For now, my job is to guard the bed you arrived in, to stand between it and the entrance to the tunnel. The princess will not ride it again until a decision is made. Perhaps she will never leave this box canyon. It is one suggestion already put before the council of horses."

Precious whined.

"Why did you bring me here? I just wanted to ride a horse of a different color. We are getting deeper and deeper into this unknown place. There's no way home. We lost the way you knew. It sounds like I am a prisoner of the horses. What will become of me?"

Dreamer was unflustered. His voice was calm.

"Talking Horse will keep us from harm. He only restrains you until the other horses are assured of their own safety. They never proceed to a course of action until at least three viable and different solutions to a problem have been proposed. As often is the case, when three proposals are heard, more ideas come tumbling head over heels to them."

Talking Horse took a bite of grass..

"When horses have chewed and digested the grass inside a circle of hesitation and it is time to move on to un-grazed pasture, the decision will be made quickly and cooperatively and with little or no effort to persuade one another. Horses believe that in the silence of grazing, a wise decision makes itself known to them—in their coming together places like Storytelling Place."

Dreamer looked at Precious. She had a quizzical look on her face— as if she couldn't believe it.

He said, "Talking Horse has been so happy to talk to someone that he has been telling me Horsestories and one day—I am still astonished, every time I think about it— I thought I saw a tear in his eye as he told me a story my grandmother told me. I recognized it as soon as I heard it."

"I suppose that story about a princess who couldn't keep a secret is partly responsible for the horses guessing you are a princess. You certainly aren't dressed like a princess. But, your long blonde hair is just like the princess in the story."

Precious frowned and stomped her foot.

"Horse lore has brought them information—a picture of a princess—but what about their reasoning? I know there are princesses with short hair and some with dark hair too; aren't you worried about how horses think?"

Dreamer shook his head.

"No, Horse information gathering and processing may be different from ours but when they remember one of *The Stories*, the structure of the story somehow fits the situation and connects the horses to what might need to be known in that moment."

"Although your long blonde hair alerted them to the princess story, it must have been the scout of the council of horses who, then, observed you and reported that you might be a princess who couldn't keep a secret. Now, I am beginning to see why we didn't find the horses right away. They were avoiding us, waiting for the scout's report."

Precious sighed.

"The box canyon might be a safe place for horses but what about me? Will I ever ride a horse of a different color? I don't have anything in common with a Sharpie and I can't imagine telling horse secrets to that bird. How can horses imagine I would get close enough to that monstrous bird to say anything to it?"

The earth trembled. Precious and Dreamer heard a metallic ring.

Talking Horse twitched his ears.

"Sounds like rocks falling—a cave in, maybe somewhere in the tunnel. Sounds like detritus falling on the metal path."

Precious sat down on the ground. Tears filled her eyes and she sobbed into her own fingers.

A young and curious colt had been watching Precious all this time. He was inching closer to her despite warnings from the mothers. The colt was pure white—coat and mane— except for a rusty spot that surrounded one eye. He walked up behind, Precious and pushed against her back with his soft nose.

Precious turned around and bumped noses with the colt. She was startled to be looking into the depths of a huge dark eye. She caught her breath and didn't say a word—just stared at the spot around the colt's eye. It reminded her of something— but what, she couldn't quite remember.

Talking Horse said to Precious, " Colt has taken a liking to you. Ask for permission to ride. Colt will take you to a better place—to Storytelling Place."

Precious looked at Dreamer. He nodded his head.

"Yes, go on without me. I'll join you later. Talking Horse and I must see about repairs to the tunnel."

"Take me to a storytelling place. I am going to ride on your back," said Precious as she tried to mount the colt.

When Colt heard her words, he began to stamp his feet and back up and go forward and Precious could not mount him.

"That is not a proper request; it does not take the colts wishes into consideration," said Talking Horse. "See how the colt thwarts you. Are princesses not as well taught as our youngest foals?"

"You must find words of permission and cooperation before you may ride a horse of a different color or a curious colt," Dreamer reminded Precious.

Precious was baffled. Didn't know what to do.

"*She needs some help,*" Dreamer whispered to Talking Horse.

"I'll give you a hint," said the horse. "Start out with *I want to* –Put *can you* or *will you* in the middle and end with: *Thank you. It is done.*"

Precious hesitated for a moment and then she whispered in Colt's ear.

"I want to go to a storytelling place. Can you, will you help me?"

As Precious said, "*Will you?*" Colt threw back his head and reared up on hind legs. He landed back on four feet and stood perfectly still.

"In horse talk that means, I'm glad you asked and let's go," said Talking Horse.

"Thank you, thank you," said Precious with enthusiasm. "It is done. We are on our way to a storytelling place."

Dreamer and Talking Horse galloped back to the secret tunnel.

Dreamer's voice was fading but she heard him say.

"Learn to recognize the colt's body signals; communicate with the colt you are riding. We'll be together again at Storytelling Place."

At the entrance to Magic Bed Tunnel, Dreamer dismounted and walked beside Talking Horse. They looked into the tunnel together.

"The metal path is blocked, some boulders still rolling," said the horse.

"Yes, I hear the ring of metal. It could be dangerous to enter the tunnel."

"It may be more dangerous not to enter the tunnel," said Talking Horse. "We must clear the way at least to Turning Point."

"What is this Turning Point?"

"You'll see when we get there," said the horse. "You have passed by it many times while you slept."

On the other side of the tunnel, while Talking Horse and Dreamer were working to remove debris, late afternoon was growing clouds. The sky was streaked pale yellow and grey. A trembling earth disturbed the monstrous bird's napping dreams about the Land of Wizards.

One eye opened. The Sharpie twisted her neck and cocked her head and listened.

Metal ringing—like the wake up warning— dinging. No, it is not here—that annoying sound. Nothing to fear. Bad dream—

Tomorrow, metal will be found. Go back to sleep. It's all right. No hovering tonight, everything out of sight—clouds cover the moon. No light—morning comes too soon.

She blinked and fell asleep again, perched in the mouth of her cave so that morning sun would waken her. Next morning she lifted her wings and soared down the mountain path toward what was still ringing in her ears. The sound like a sound in the Land of Wizards.

I'm beautiful there.

Suddenly she screamed, "Aaasssccccceeeeiiim"

How? Now? Unroll a bit of scroll? What am I remembering? Why did he scream, wait—WAIT?

The bird cocked her head, looked around and up to the clouds as if she might see it written there.

Mirror, mirror on the wall—A magic potion bitter as gall—Running waters lift the screen—Transformation can be seen.

It was no longer mysterious to her—the rhyme written on a fragment of Onemug's ancient scroll. She dropped her head a little, stared out into space, cocked her head to the left and craned her neck. It looked like she was hearing him. But she was remembering.

Wait, wait—don't swallow so much. One drop on the tip of the tongue reveals a secret better won in another dimension where powers need not be tame. Don't forget! Remember your name.

She shook her head and extended her claws to stay awake. Riding and gliding on drafts of mountain air, entranced her. Going back to her perch in the cozy cave seemed enticing but hunger was making itself known to the bird. She remembered.

Gold somewhere on this path.

The glint from a metal ring in the side of the mountain caught her eye. She landed on the path. The tip of one toe curled thru the ring. She pulled. The door to Magic Bed Tunnel creaked. She was clutching the ring, pulling harder, bracing one foot against the mountain, flapping her wings and pulling again and again. A door screeched open.

"I will have it. Whatever is inside is mine!"

The Mysterious Chicket

As Colt carried Precious away from Dreamer and Talking Horse, Precious began to worry.

WHAT IF Dreamer is trapped in the tunnel?
WHAT IF I am left in this place all alone?
WHAT IF the colt doesn't take me to a safe place?
Dreamer SHOULD NOT have left me.
And I SHOULD NOT have–
WHY DID I listen to Dreamer?
HE SHOULD NOT be listening to a talking horse.

Precious pulled on the colts mane to turn it back but it ignored her.

"Turn Around!" she shouted, but Colt did not respond to her command and kept on trotting toward a favorite storytelling place.

Colt stayed close to the mountainside. They came to a place where trees and shrubs made an almost impenetrable thicket. Colt skirted around the thicket following the edge of tangled growth around and around.

Precious was sleepy. Her eye lids felt heavy. Her back and shoulders were beginning to ache. She was hungry and wondering why she ever wanted to ride a horse of a different color. Colt made a sharp turn and jostled her. She blinked her eyes. And in that moment she realized, she and the colt were entering a clearing—thicket all around them.

I don't remember going thru the thicket; how did we get here?

At the inside edge of the thicket there were thorn bushes and vines all heavily laden with fruit—black berries, a heavily seeded fruit; red heart shaped fruit with barely visible seeds; blue and purple smooth skinned fruits with no visible outside seeds.

Colt was gingerly mouthing some berries of a saw-tooth thorn bush as Precious dismounted. Precious ate some of the heart shaped fruit.

Where they were standing, the clearing was carpeted by a thick and spongy moss-like growth. There were tiny elegant white flowers sprinkled through it. Off center, closer to the far side of the clearing, four huge rocks stood like sentinels at the four corners of a square bed of gravel.

In the middle of the gravel, what looked like a stack of flat rocks formed a pedestal for a circular earthen container. Precious heard the sound of water bubbling. Water sprayed into the air and filled and cascaded over the sides of the earthen container.

Colt ran over to the gravel bed and stamped his front feet. He made a depression in the gravel and drank from it. In her cupped hands, Precious caught water coming over the sides of the earthen container and drank too.

"Ah, it is refreshing here," said Precious. "Light comes from above. The light is sooooo soft—filtered through leaves of trees and vines overhead. No glaring here. This must be Storytelling Place."

Precious decided to mount the colt again but whenever she approached close enough to touch Colt, he backed away from her.

Precious grumbled.

"Well I didn't really want to ride you right now anyway. I am so tired; going to take a nap. Please don't wander too far away from me. I need your help to survive in this strange place."

Colt threw his head back.

"I hope that means you will help me."

Precious laid her head down on a cushion of moss and just before she fell asleep she remembered.

"Thank you. It is done."

Back at the tunnel, rumbling had ceased. Talking Horse pulled Magic Bed deep into the tunnel again. Dreamer was loading rocks into it— clearing the metal path back toward the valley of horses. When it was filled up with rocks, Dreamer lifted the log and Magic Bed traveled by gravity to the box canyon again. Talking Horse and Dreamer followed it.

"The back-side of the bed can be released," said the horse. "Turn the handle."

Dreamer turned a handle and the back side of the bed swung open like a door. Rocks tumbled out on the ground.

Then Talking Horse positioned himself in front of Magic Bed and leaned against a padded board, a yoke that was attached to the front of the bed by another board. As the horse walked, the bed moved up the path again.

Dreamer asked, "Are you bruised by the yoke?"

"No, just a feeling of pressure and heaviness in the chest."

Horse and Dreamer worked long into the night and deeper into the tunnel. Finally Dreamer set the brake and Talking Horse stepped out of the yoke. They fell asleep—Dreamer resting his head against the bed, Talking Horse standing beside him. They were wakened by a creaking metallic sound and a screech. There was a vibration in the metal path. Dreamer put his ear to the metal.

"It sounds like scratching."

"We are almost at Turning Point," said the horse. "A few more rocks to remove—"

Dreamer lifted a huge rock and placed it in the bed. He pushed another large boulder to the side of the tunnel and off the metal path.

As the boulder rolled out of the way, the horse said, "There it is— Turning Point. Feel the warm breeze. Smell the fragrance of fruit."

"I do smell it and I am hungry," said Dreamer.

The horse stepped to one side of the entrance to Turning Point.

"Go ahead. I'll follow you. Feel the ground beneath your feet. Reach out into the blackest blackness. Feel the sides of the tunnel. You'll find it. You'll come to the Crystal Chamber."

"How far is it?" asked Dreamer.

"Not far. We can follow our noses. The fragrance of fruit will guide us. I tried to get to the fruit one day, by myself but that hallway is not tall enough for a horse to travel the whole length. The way narrows but you can go farther than I went—maybe get to where the breeze enters. There is a warm glow to follow. You may be the one who can reach fruit at the other end of the tunnel."

A Crystal Chamber

t first the passageway was very dark and Dreamer moved cautiously on his way. Then he thought he saw light, like a circular basket, woven of light— bright pink at first and then brilliant green and electric blue pulsing like a swirling vortex.

He was awe stricken for a few moments and stood still and just stared at the light.

"Don't stop now," said Talking Horse. "Go on. Go on!"

Dreamer protested.

"I want to stay with the light."

"No, go on," said Talking Horse as he nudged Dreamer with his nose and pushed him down the path.

It wasn't far—just a little way to a magnificent, brightly lit, tall, arched chamber of pink crystal. Crystal pillars marked off entrances to corridors, multi-colored crystal hallways.

The corridors were not all pink. Dreamer noticed a golden one nearby. As soon as Dreamer set foot in the chamber his footsteps verberated some crystals and they seemed to whisper—*footsteps.*

"What was that?"

As Dreamer said, *what,* he heard it echo first in one ear and then a few moments later in his other ear. By the time he said, *was that,* the reverberation struck crystals and they sang out a song and put notes to his words. They kept repeating until he heard two *what's* and *musical notes* in one ear and at the same time he heard, *was that* and *musical notes* in his other ear.

Dreamer covered his ears with his hands and looked up at the ceiling of the chamber.

Perhaps the dancing lights and the light in this chamber come from above.

He looked around and saw multi- colored light streaming into the chamber from many hallways.

There is light everywhere.

Talking Horse said nothing, just stood beside Dreamer and sniffed the fragrance of fruit coming from that one hallway he knew he couldn't go down.

The whole chamber was so large Dreamer had a feeling it would take more than one day just to cross it. He looked at Talking Horse and whispered.

"Are there too many hallways to explore in one lifetime?"

Precious woke to a sound like wind chime notes—a crystal clear sound. She thought she heard the word, *footsteps,* whispered.

"I must be dreaming," she said to Colt who was grazing nearby but then she heard it again.

It sounded like, *What was*—and musical notes. It seemed to be coming from behind the fountain. Precious walked around the fountain and the colt followed close behind her.

"Look at the containers piled here around the fountain—piles and piles of baskets and some so tightly woven they might carry water. I wonder who left them here?"

Behind the fountain was a rock face pushing its way out of the thicket on the mountainside. Precious almost laughed.

Old Man in the Mountain looks like he has lost his nose.

As Precious stood there, looking at the huge formation she heard musical notes again and sounds like whispering. It was coming from a mouth-like formation. The closer she came to it, the harder it was to see inside the mouth.

Colt was following Precious. She looked back at him.

" It is going to be too high for me to reach by myself. Please, please— I would like to look into that mouth cave. I will need to stand on your back to do it. Will you help me?"

Colt threw his head back and stood perfectly still. Precious climbed up on the colt's back and carefully balanced herself. She took a few deep breaths. She crouched on her feet and waited until her foothold felt secure and then when she was relaxed, she stood up and reached for the cave.

"Thank you, thank you," she said to the colt. "It is done."

Precious reached into the cave. She found a crevice in a rock to hold onto and pulled herself up and into Mouth Cave.

Light dancing at the back of the cave—and a tunnel.

Precious spoke gently to Colt.

" I am going to explore a tunnel. Please wait for me."

Precious heard music again and started crawling down the tunnel toward it. The tunnel grew wider. There was more and more head room. She was standing on her own two feet when she came to the pink chamber.

Precious stopped and gazed into wondrous, crystallized space. When she let her breath out, there was a faint chime-like whisper.

Dreamer was wondering whether to go straight across the chamber or to take a turn down a hallway when he heard the chime-like sound.

Dreamer glanced to his left. He didn't know whether to believe his eyes or not. There stood Precious, not far away—at the entrance to a hallway.

He called out.

"Precious!"

The verberation crystals answered, *Precious*, and the reverberation crystals sang a song that came from her name until it echoed in the chamber.

Dreamer's whole body seemed to pulsate with the sounds. Precious listened and didn't speak. She just waved to Dreamer. Dreamer and Talking Horse headed towards Precious. No one spoke again until they entered the hallway to Storytelling Place.

A few steps into the hallway, they spoke in whispers. "How did you get here?" asked Dreamer.

"By ear. I was asleep at what must be the horses' Storytelling Place, when music wakened me and when I tried to find where the sound was coming from, I noticed it seemed to be coming from a mouth-like opening to a cave in the mountain."

"I followed the tunnel at the back of the cave to this place. What did you find out about the falling rocks in Magic Bed Tunnel? And how did you get here?"

Precious had so many questions but the horse interrupted their conversation.

" Excuse me but could you bring me some food from Storytelling Place. I am hungry and I know I can't get there from here. The tunnel is already brushing my ears."

"Yes, yes, I found baskets by a fountain. We can bring you food and water," Precious said as she started back down the tunnel to Storytelling Place.

Dreamer was following behind her, telling her: Talking Horse calls the hallway into the central crystal chamber, Turning Point Hallway. He insisted we must clear Magic Bed Tunnel to Turning Point.

He nudged me down the dark tunnel, until I found my way to the inner crystal light and that's how we got here.

So many hallways lead from this central pink chamber. There may be undiscovered ways out of the box canyon, ways to enter the outside world again. There might be a way to leave the valley of horses undetected by the Sharpie.

The Box Canyon entrance to Magic Bed Tunnel is cleared to Turning Point. But, we didn't clear the tunnel all the way back to the Valley of Horses.

We heard some strange sounds on the other side of the cave-in— digging and scratching sounds like someone or something has opened the metal door.

Talking Horse was standing just a few feet from the crystal cavern—a little way into Mouth Cave tunnel. He watched Dreamer and Precious approach Storytelling Place. They were crawling most of the way until they came to Mouth Cave.

Precious and Dreamer were glad to be able to stand up again and stretch.

"There's the colt," said Precious.

When Colt heard her voice it stood quietly under the opening to the cave and waited.

Dreamer stepped out of the cave first and onto the colt's back. He stood on the ground by Colt and helped Precious get sure footing on Colt's back and then helped her step down to the ground again.

They ate fruit and drank from the fountain. Precious and Dreamer sat down on soft springy moss and just rested for a few minutes.

"It's a blessing for Talking Horse that someone left these baskets here," said Precious.

As she moved toward the baskets they both heard the sounds of galloping horses.

"The mothers and colts are coming," said Dreamer. "It must be storytelling time and time to consider how they might protect themselves from you."

Dreamer hurriedly filled one basket with fruit and another with water from the fountain.

"I'll take these to Talking Horse. He and I will explore another hallway."

Colt could hardly stand still long enough for Dreamer to stand on his back and enter the cave.

As soon as Dreamer was inside the cave again, he shouted to Precious.

"The horses have some important decisions to make. They must have called the cricket to tell a story that can help them. Listen, there may be some clues about escaping the box canyon. When cricket starts to tell the story, breathe in rhythm with the chirps. You will understand—breathing together."

Precious protested.

"I don't want to stay here. I'm afraid. Too many horses! What will become of me?"

"Stay with the colt," said Dreamer. "You are in a safe place. We'll be back. I'll come for you soon. Experience Storytelling Place. There is much to learn. Hear— now. "

Storytelling Place

Dreamer left Storytelling Place behind him. He knew Talking Horse would be patiently waiting for him, at the end of the tunnel. He could see his dark form outlined in the glow from the pink central chamber in the mountain.

Colt bolted for his favorite place to stand—close to the fountain and close to the storytelling cricket.

Precious followed Colt and stood beside him in the semi-circle of horses.

The cricket began to chirp. At first, Precious didn't understand one word and then she relaxed and began to breathe in rhythm with the cricket's chirps. and then she heard what the cricket was saying.

"So you want a story about keeping secrets and about leaving the valley of horses— about escaping but, you do not want the tale of the king who kept his own daughter, captive in a dungeon."

"Ahhhhh, haaaaa, what basket shall I read today? What is woven into this pretty tartan work of art?"

"*Oh, oh,*" thought Precious.

"What have we done disturbing the baskets, removing two of them. Will the cricket notice? Will the mothers notice what is missing? And if they notice what will they do to me?"

She stepped a little closer to Colt and tried to make herself invisible as the cricket was saying:

There is a Turning Point and a central pink chamber where escape is possible.

Once upon a time a great wizard from another time lived at the end of a tunnel that connects to the pink central chamber. From that crystal chamber, anyone can get to Turning Point Tunnel and from there to Magic Bed Tunnel and into this valley.

Now, I don't know exactly how the wizard found this crystal chamber but this basket reminds me—he lived in a cave, a short distance from the monstrous Sharpie's cave.

I saw him watching the Sharpie and waiting—waiting for something to happen. He laid out something for the Sharpie. I guess it was food for a Sharpie.

The wizard didn't stay long; was apt to disappear in a few minutes right before my eyes. Many times he had a frown on his face and a tear in his eye as if he were very, very disappointed.

One day I ventured into the Wizard's cave and watched and watched and waited and waited in a safe niche in the side of the cave. He appeared when I had almost fallen asleep.

I was in a dreamy state—chirping a slow steady dreamy chirp. The wizard heard me. He looked at me and said, *"Ahhhhh haaaaa ahhh hhha,"* in the same rhythm as my chirps.

We were beginning to understand one another. He sensed my fear of him and I sensed that he really didn't want to hurt me—was just curious about me. When I knew for sure he wouldn't hurt me, when I felt safe, I relaxed and almost fell asleep to his *ah ha's* and my own chirps.

But, I was curious about him and forced myself to stay awake to watch him. The wizard's nose scrunched up; his eyebrows rose. His eyes looked up and to the right, as if he were searching for or creating an image.

He turned his head to one side—to the right and lowered his gaze to ear level as if he were searching for a sound or creating a voice.

I almost fell out of my niche when he whispered.

"*I need to know a little more about where I am and you can help me. Thank you. It is done.*"

I perked up my ears at that and chirped back.

"How do you know the secret to this horse valley—the secret to getting my cooperation and to getting the cooperation of the horses that dwell here?"

The wizard rubbed his leg like I was rubbing my leg and he said, "*I didn't know that I knew—that secret.*"

"Well," I said. "You might not know you know—but you know more than you know you know. How did you get here? How do you disappear?"

" I'm not sure I know," he said.

It all seems like a dream to me. I was looking for a way to escape pollution. I had a passion about transforming matter back into pure energy. We might have abundance then, for everyone. We might all live together peacefully, non-violently.

Suddenly, I was transported here; I don't know how. What I remember of my experience here is in bits and pieces I'm trying to sew together. It isn't whole and it isn't something I can wear comfortably until the pieces come together for me—like my patchwork robe.

I don't know how I am finding these scrolls. One I found in a cave was pointed out to me *in a dream*. Just like I know that we are communicating to one another, I know that what I read on that scroll was a lullaby.

The lullaby told about a lost formula, the magic Ynnaline. By some kind of coincidence, not long after I read the scroll, I found a mysterious bottle labeled Ynnaline, with just a few drops of *magic* inside it. I tasted its strange liquidness.

"I saw the Wizard open his mouth. His tongue touched his upper lip and then he rolled it around to his lower lip as if he were tasting something. He shook his head from side to side before he spoke again."

The effects of the formula on me and on another were strange. It was as if we were liquidness—influenced by intention in another dimension.

"The wizard's voice was so low at times, it was as if he were speaking to himself. Then he spoke in a firm tone of voice to me."

Some unknown principles prevail here, in this dimension. I hope that when I understand them, I might understand what happened to me and I might be able to change what the drops did to the other one who tasted them.

"I strummed a few chirps and then asked Onemug, *Do you think what's in the bottle could be a kind of medicine?* The wizard stroked his beard."

Ynnaline, yes, perhaps it might be a kind of medicine. What it can do seems like magic in my world—perhaps in any world. I thought, I hoped it might release us from our fears.

"*You, the great Wizard, didn't know there is no escape, no running away from fear that there is confronting it and tapping into it—accepting it and going thru it or looking at it in another dimension?* I chirped at him in astonishment."

The Wizard shook his head from side to side. He looked up to the right and to the left. He told me created images and remembered images were flooding into his consciousness. I chirped his name and called him back to himself. He blinked and then he looked straight ahead. He was listening and silent for a few moments—breathing with me, just breathing.

When he spoke again, he whispered.

"*So much I didn't know—Didn't know until someone else tasted the formula. I didn't know that a monster, a Sharpie could be created here.*"

A tear came to his eye. Then he spoke with a kind of groan.

"In that other part of my life, experiments led to deadly mushroom explosions."

Onemug shook his head back and forth again and looked down at his feet.

After the Sharpie materialized, I had this heavy feeling in my chest and in my hands and feet ——a kind of sadness I had not known before.

I asked myself, *Why? Why did I decide to work with that formula? Can it be kept secret from those who might misuse it? Do I dare use it, when so much about it still surprises me?*

I still believe it is possible to bring worldly formulas and other-worldly formulas into agreement—to find a Unified Field Theory. Even if our disastrous mistakes cannot be avoided, I hope that one day they might be repaired.

Onemug assumed a strange stance, raised his bent elbows away from his body. His elbows were bobbing up and down. He looked like a bird undecided about staying or taking flight. His hands were clenched into fists and he groaned.

My anxiety became a heaviness that grew almost intolerable and I thought I would have to run away—get out of here. But then, I remembered to take slow deep breaths.

From somewhere deep inside myself, I heard a voice: *Your feet are heavy, heavy—too heavy to run. There is nowhere to go and there is much to be won by staying and going deeper, deeper. Parlaying here and there, you are the one to go deeper because you care. You can wake the sleeper and dare—to go deeper –deeper. You can bring everywhere and every when –all together again.*

Onemug was silent then for such a long time, I wondered if he was ever going to speak again.

I was about to fall asleep when he said, "The first drop of Ynnaline I tasted was so bitter I had trouble swallowing it and then it was unbelievable the acceleration I experienced—like riding a beam of light."

"*Were you here or there*? I asked him.

"Maybe here and there. I don't know."

I hung onto whatever was moving me as if my life depended upon it. Now when it happens, the acceleration is not so frightening –just a surprise. I ride it out, overcome my mixed feelings and accept ecstasy and agony in the same moment. I have survived it now, many times and I have gone on to amazing next adventures.

"How long did you ride the beam of light?" I asked Onemug.

"Each time I go thru my own fear, that part of the ride seems shorter and shorter and I don't know how long it was the first time—maybe a life time before I began to wonder, to open my eyes, and discover more about myself in this place."

"Are those normal feelings?" I asked Onemug.

He began to mumble and seemed to be talking to himself.

At mid-life, somewhere close to our 40th year, biologists have discovered there is an opening of new circuits—new connections made in the brain.

It can be as challenging as adolescence. Glad I read about it and recognized my mid-life crisis emotions. No wonder it can call forth enigmatic changes in a life. And there is research that supports the notion there is another change-of-life time.

Reputable scientists are now saying there is a lesser but still noticeable gain in brain connections again between the 60th and 70th years. It is what the ancients might have called an initiation—a kind of death to the old self but a beginning again.

In our later years, having the resources to go thru our fears we can let go of the past and begin again. Both times can be dangerous times, accompanied by intense feelings, anxiety and confusion. A person might think his reactions are abnormal—might think he is going crazy.

Suddenly he remembered my question and he raised his voice.

"Yes, it is normal."

And then he fell into a contemplative silence and I heard his rambling again.

Tapping into it—holistic intelligence! Isn't that genius, allowing new connections—veils cleared away—recognizing our inbuilt programming—becoming conscious of a higher purpose?

It was more than coincidence, more than luck to find and to read the research papers about ancient methods of healing using meridians—energy pathways in the body.

When I told my friends about the research they still wouldn't believe me—that tapping certain points on the body, can clear away blocked energies at places along the meridians where trauma—mental or physical— has caused a kind of short circuit in the balanced flow that is health.

Since they won't believe documented research on esoteric healing I'm almost certain they will not believe me if I tell them what I have learned in this place—that a person can live more than one lifetime in a lifetime. I must have enough presence of mind to keep quiet about my experiences.

"It sounds a little like horse-sense to me," I encouraged Onemug.

Onemug closed his eyes and sat quietly for a little while. His voice was so soft it barely reached my ears.

Horse-feathers –wonder where that thought came from? From a feeling that I'm just not cantering along? I seem to be flying nowhere and it is beastly out of control— this mid-life winging it –leaping and soaring into other dimensions

There was a prolonged silence.

Then Onemug looked me in the eye and spoke in a hesitant, tentative tone.

"Here I am— listening to a cricket,—exploring a mysterious valley and yet I haven't let go of my traditional thinking. That I can leap into another dimension and soar still seems dauntingly impossible to the old me. I have to stop myself from trying to dismiss the evidence of my own experiences."

"Tell me about leaping and soaring," I chirped. Onemug's voice regained its timbre and he spoke to me as if he were speaking to an old friend—telling his story.

At first, I was thirsty and searching for water—so thirsty that I was soaring down, down toward a broad, rather calm river. A reflection rippling in the water below me looked like an eagle.

I thought it was strange—the reflection. But I didn't stop to wonder how I was swooping down and drinking without ever touching the ground. Then I was up–up–again and soaring and then I was tired, so very tired. I searched for a place to rest.

There were tears in my eyes. I was only part way up the mountain when my feet touched ground. I didn't know why I was sad—maybe because I was tired, so very tired. My whole body felt heavy. I closed my eyes.

No more distraction. Good to be alone with myself.

I don't know if I slept. I remember blinking and then looking around. I found myself in a hollow space surrounded by stones. Finally it dawned on me—I was in a cave!

"Were you an eagle then?" I asked Onemug.

He continued on with his story.

On the dark ledge in front of the cave, there was a shallow pool of water. The moon was reflecting in it. I hesitated. Should I take a closer look at the reflections in that shallow pool? A wizard with a long white beard—wearing a patched robe and a pointed hat stared back at me.

"You look like a wizard to me," I said.

The wizard's voice dropped again and he was mumbling.

Even after all my trips to this place. Visiting this realm, breathing with a cricket, I still have doubts. Am I really here-talking to a cricket?

I heard what he said even though he was just talking to himself.

I stepped out to the edge of my niche and chirped as loud as I could, "You are talking to a cricket."

I think I reassured him.

He shook his head and whispered, "*Yes, Yes, but who in my world would believe one word I said, if I told them about you?*"

I asked him, "How long will you stay, Halbert?"

That's what he said his first name was in that other world he came from. He looked down at his patched robe, rubbed his hand over some stitching on one sleeve before he answered me.

"I don't know. There may be answers to my yearnings here. I might find some answers in ancient manuscripts. I might find maps. I might uncover forgotten formulas. I haven't found what I'm looking for in likely places and so why not try unlikely places?"

"My studies at the university are just theoretical until proven. What we in science are trying to prove with our theories, doesn't always match what I experience here."

"Reverses, paradoxes—I would not have believed the laws of physics might differ between dimensions if I hadn't traveled this way. Can anyone tie it all together—spiritual mysteries of the universe and physics? Can we find home again?"

Colt whinnied and flicked his ears and interrupted the story telling. He was transmitting.

"How does that story help us?"

The cricket rubbed its legs together a few times and adjusted its chirps to the swish of the colt's tail.

"It doesn't but it might be of some use to a princess. If she can disappear to another dimension like the Wizard does, the horses will not have to keep her here—will not have to worry about her giving away their secrets to a Sharpie."

Precious was watching Colt's mother and she began to breathe in rhythm with the mother's breaths so that she could hear what Colt's mother was saying to him. Precious wasn't surprised to hear the mother's thoughts.

So, it seems we are to help the princess find the Wizard and help the Wizard know what he doesn't know he knows so he can take the princess to his world with him.

"No! I don't want to go to another world I don't know anything about, with a man I don't know anything about. It is strange enough here."

She took a deep breath and sighed and sighed and almost cried, "I am a princess. I was safe in Castletown. Everyone in Castletown is protected by my mother and father and by their rules."

Then she was sobbing.

"Dreamer! Colt! Protect me! Oh why? Why did I ever leave my home?"

Tears spilled down her cheeks.

Colt was watching Precious and he was moved by her tears. He nudged her with his soft nose and looked into her eyes and tossed his head to one side. Somehow Precious knew Colt was leading her away from the semi-circle of horses and away from her fears and her tears.

Colt coaxed Precious to follow him and without really paying any attention to where they were going, Precious followed the colt onto a brambly path.

Cricket's chirping stopped. It watched Colt and Precious leave Storytelling Place. They disappeared around a corner of underbrush.

Cricket took a few moments to contemplate the empty space of their leaving. It was silent—staring at the place of disappearance.

There was a hushed expectant silence at Storytelling Place. Horses stopped munching grass. They lifted their heads. They twitched their ears and stared at Cricket.

"Is that the end of the story?" a black and white horse transmitted, as it flicked its tail and looked around at the other horses.

"I don't know how the story ends," said Cricket. "We are all now a part of the story and we must see it through to whatever happens."

Mother's began explaining to their colts:

Our secret way to the valley and to the mountain caves above where the Sharpie and the Wizard dwell is blocked by falling rocks and big boulders. That's why we have come to Storytelling Place—to find some answers.

We must hope that Dreamer and Talking Horse can bring us good news. If they can clear Magic Bed Tunnel to Turning Point, there is a chance a back door may be found to the Wizard's cave and to the valley. They may find a way to take the princess to the outside world again.

Horses and colts began to mill around and whinny. Cricket called out to them.

"There is more than hope of escaping this box canyon. At Storytelling Place there is knowing the way; and there is remembering a story."

A Grandmother Horsestory

Cricket began to tell the restless horses another story and they gathered around the fountain.

Once upon a time, a grandmother horse told me she found Turning Point Tunnel. She entered the tunnel and went on until she reached a central cavern. But she didn't enter or go on because, a wizard appeared there in the middle of the chamber.

He was mumbling to himself. His voice echoed and set the crystals singing. It was unbearable noise to her. Her ears were ringing and she quickly turned around.

Grandmother horse knew the wizard hadn't come to the chamber through the mountain door or through the secret passageway.

The door to the valley was locked from the inside because Magic Bed was tight against the door. She knew if the Wizard didn't come through that door, there must be another way in and out of our valley—perhaps another way somehow connected to that noisy central cavern.

She whinnied that message to her grandcolt.

Onemug comes and goes. He hasn't made his home here but he must have found a place to rest, down one of the central chamber's many hallways.

A colt at Storytelling Place stamped her feet and looked at cricket. She was throwing her head to one side.

Cricket understood what she was asking.

No, Halebert did not draw me a map but he did describe where he has been—told me stories so that I might recognize similar places when I come to them. It's as if he expects, one day I'll find myself in his incredibly strange dimension.

A black and white horse, whinnied and shook its head. Cricket stopped chirping and heard its questioning.

Has Onemug found the baskets by the fountain? Does he know the sacred horsestory of Fair Maiden and a cricket? Is that why Onemug thought a cricket might help him?

The horse was trying to connect Cricket's stories and the grandmother horsestory to its own sense of horsestory.

Cricket chirped.

"Perhaps there is another golden thread for this cricket to carry somewhere. Could the thread be Onemug's story? One day you will make the connection when you need to know."

Cricket resumed story telling.

Unbelievable wonders—wonders you might not guess exist can best be described at Storytelling Place.

Stories find invisible stepping stones just under the surface—just like what's hidden in a river's rushing flow— stepping stones that will allow us to cross deep waters and to find a safe shoreline.

The waves, the rapids, what bubbles up in a story becomes familiar to us so life at the edge of a river on a rampage is not so daunting.

When we have story eyes and ears we can see and hear endless possibilities—and then there are no insurmountable barriers.

A black and white horse whinnied its affirmation.

Cricket heard a familiar chorus of horse sense coming from the whole group of horses.

Stories are not just for the sake of our future generations. Stories are for horses, wizards, crickets, princes and princesses, for anyone, for everyone. The right story at the right time takes us where we need to go.

Our horsestories tell us, when we stumble, we know we need to pick up our hooves and move on—or flap our wings if we're a cricket. We must get to where we can see the bigger picture.

Suddenly, storytelling was done and grazing on the grass of contemplation had begun. The horses were digesting what had been transmitted and received. All agreed there was nothing to do but wait and see what Talking Horse and Dreamer might discover.

The Golden Glow

When Colt's mother looked up she didn't see her colt or Precious anywhere. Precious was frowning and shuffling her feet and so many tears were streaming out of her eyes she didn't really pay any attention to where her steps were taking her when she and the colt left storytelling place.

She just followed Colt down a brambly path and into the thicket again. She was surprised when Colt turned a corner in the thicket and brought her to a golden clearing.

The whole clearing had a golden glow. In the middle of the clearing there was a golden lake. Silver sparkles were sweeping across it. Precious approached the mysterious lake and looked into it.

She saw strange reflections—black horses, white horses— just like the horses the horse seller had brought to her father's kingdom.

She could see tournaments in Castletown. Her father, the king, and her mother, the queen were giving orders to the pages, to the warriors, to the guards at the gates and it looked like nothing had changed in Castletown. It was just as she left it. How long ago, she did not know.

Colt was grazing on luscious tender grass that grew round the lake. He was wandering farther and farther away from the homesick and puzzled princess.

Precious sat down by the lake. She shook her head and blinked her eyes and pinched herself. She brushed her long blonde hair away from her eyes. She couldn't believe what she was seeing in the lake.

Where is my reflection?

She leaned over the bank, closer and closer to the water, trying to see her own reflection in the water but it was not there—only pictures of Castletown and her mother and father.

Precious leaned even closer. Her nose was touching the water when she fell into the golden lake head first. Precious was caught in an undertow—a kind of whirling, pulling, magnetic force that pulled her in deeper and deeper.

She was holding her breath and she became more and more frightened. She didn't know how to swim or even that she might struggle against the current, against the swirling water. She surrendered to it and was taken deeper—falling deeper and deeper. Her mind raced.

What makes the water golden? How can there be so much water here? How can it be so forceful? Why didn't I know it might be dangerous?

She closed her eyes and in an ever so slow motion—heels over head— she somersaulted under the golden water drifting deeper and deeper.

I have believed all my life that sweet water is scarce. The effort, the drudgery to haul water up from our deep wells. How can there be so much water here? If Castletown only knew—

Her thoughts were floating, slowing down, moving in slow motion like her body.

If only I could tell them about the lake and its sweet golden water— enough to drown in.

She opened her eyes.

Deep—too deep to reach the surface but I must take a breath or I will die.

Her chest felt like fire and there was a lump in her throat that hurt. She grabbed herself around her legs and curled into a ball.

Dreamer! I must take a breath and drown!

Suddenly strands of her long hair were swirling, pulled away from her head. She was whirled, caught up in a pulling current and swooshed into a crystal clear dome at the bottom of the lake. She took a breath.

Air! Where am I?

She stretched her arms above her head.

What kind of structure is this? Fresh, fragrant air, spicy hint of lavender, cinnamon—

She was being warmed and her clothes were drying in the circulating atmosphere of a strange dome.

Middle of something—not enough space to stand. Transparent water-tight walls—soft, warm, golden glow around it.

She knew she was safe but still she was terrified. She began tapping on the side of her palm.

Even though I'm afraid, I accept myself without judgment.

She tapped under her eye.

This remaining fear.

She continued tapping the other healing buttons. It was calming and she remembered.

Breathe, inhale, count. one, two, three, four. Exhale, count. one, two, three, and four.

She continued to breathe in a mindful way, the way Dreamer taught her to breathe. Still she couldn't help crying out.

"Help, help me! Dreamer, help me."

She was exhausted from her fright but she was calm enough to curl up on the cushioned supportive floor of the transparent dome and close her eyes. She slept.

Precious woke up to a sudden jolt. She was being rolled, pressed into a narrowing corner. Her movements were being restricted. She held her breath. Tears streamed from her eyes. The whole dome was vibrating and moving. There was a crashing, rushing water sound.

Pushing two baskets in front of him, Dreamer was crawling down the tunnel to the central pink crystal chamber. He carried food and water from Storytelling Place.

Talking Horse was standing there at the end of the hallway, anxiously waiting for Dreamer.

"Where did you get the baskets?"

"They were piled on the backside of the fountain across from mouth cave."

Dreamer remembered the verberation and the disorienting reverberation he heard in the crystal chamber a short time ago and so when Talking Horse stepped into the chamber, he said nothing more to Talking Horse.

He just silently offered the baskets of nourishment to him. Talking Horse drank and ate his fill and when he was refreshed he moseyed across the chamber. Dreamer followed close behind him.

They were both stopping to *look*, stopping to *listen*, stopping to *sniff* the breezes in the chamber for a clue to which hallway they should choose to enter—to find the Wizard, to find a way to the valley, to find a way to the outside world again.

Dreamer and Talking Horse didn't even imagine other destinations at that moment.

Dreamer was stuck for awhile in thoughts of survival.

How am I, how are the horses, how is the princess going to survive? We must not stay prisoners of a box canyon that was only meant to keep us safe for the winter and from the Sharpie.

Talking Horse was still savoring the flavors in his mouth. He was focusing on food.

"Our secret hiding place needs a rest from us, from our constant grazing. We need green resources. The box canyon grasses must have their chance to sprout and grow again. We must find a way to move on to wider, not so crowded pastures."

Crystals were verberating and reverberating in the chamber. Dreamer whispered to Talking Horse.

"I must find a way back to the outside world again so the princess can choose to go back to Castletown or to stay with me. It must be her decision."

"What led you to this place?" Talking Horse whispered at Dreamer's ear.

Dreamer began to speak quietly, almost as if talking to himself.

It was such a long time ago. My grandmother's story, led me to this place. And now that I have found it—

Dreamer's meditation was interrupted. He thought he heard Precious calling out to him. Talking Horse stood still. His ears perked up and twitched. He turned his head and looked back at Dreamer. With a questioning wrinkle in his forehead, Dreamer gazed into the dark eyes of Talking Horse.

Talking Horse shook his head to one side. Dreamer caught the intent and they walked side by side down a broad hallway-corridor that seemed to have a golden glow at the end of it. As they came closer and closer to the golden glow Talking Horse and Dreamer heard a gurgling, rumbling sound.

The hallway was narrowing and dropping down deeper and deeper into the mountain. Suddenly they came to a sheer, steep drop-off, a wide gap and a dead end.

"Just a stone wall of mountain across the gap," said Talking Horse.

Dreamer looked down into the gap.

A small cavern below— river of bubbling golden water emitting a golden glow.

Dreamer and Talking horse stood still and listened for a clue about what to do.

Talking Horse stamped his foot.

"Dead end. Let's go back, my friend."

Dreamer shook his head.

"No, I hear Precious crying."

There was a gurgling sound again.

"We need to be still. Listening is a skill."

He looked down into the gap again. Her voice seemed to come from somewhere below. Then he noticed it—ladder-like vine at their feet. The ladder was hanging over the side of the ledge. It reached almost to the floor of the small cavern.

Dreamer patted Talking Horse and stroked his neck. "I hope you understand why I must leave you here to find what is Precious to me."

Dreamer crouched down, held tight to what seemed like a braided vine. He eased one leg over the ledge, found a foot hold and began his descent.

The intertwined vines swayed a little and made a crackling sound as he put his weight on fortuitous foot holds.

When he was about halfway down, the volume of the sound of the burbling in the chamber increased and changed to a grumbling more ominous tone. The river seemed to swell. It overflowed its rocky banks and rose into the gap. The vine ladder was swirled and pushed about on the wall of the gap. Dreamer was hanging on.

"Water! Up to my toes!" he shouted at Talking Horse.

Dreamer was about to scurry back up the ladder when the water level fell again. There was a sudden popping sound.

He looked down on a clear dome-like something, shooting out of the water, skidding across the floor of the chamber. He looked up at Talking Horse and shook his head as if to say—*What Next*?

What is?—came out of dreamer's mouth and Talking Horse answered, "An over-sized transparent clam shell. Be careful. Are you all right?"

"Yes, yes, I'm fine. There is something inside the clam shell."

"A pearl, no doubt," joked Talking Horse.

"Yes, no, it looks like— It couldn't be but it looks like Precious is inside the shell. I am going to take a closer look."

"What if the water rises again? You could be swept away! What if you don't have enough time to get to the vine when the water comes? What if the vine has been weakened by the watering? What if—"

Dreamer interrupted Talking Horse.

"Stop! Stop that! Your fears are talking."

"I am just looking out for you, Dreamer"

"I know. That is commendable. I'll be as careful as I can be. Thank you for your good intention. It is done."

"What is done?" asked Talking Horse.

"The deeper intention that your behavior shows to me."

"I didn't know I had a deeper intention," said the horse. "But now that I think about it, I just want to—"

Talking Horse turned around inside himself. The expression on his face—his eyes seemed to soften and it took a few moments before he said, "feel safe and peaceful and stand beside you in this place."

"Don't struggle with your fears, Talking Horse."

Dreamer paused a few more moments to reassure Talking Horse about what he knew but didn't know he knew and then Dreamer continued in a gentle tone of voice, speaking softly, slowly.

"You already have peacefulness— oneness inside you. Some say it is a core state of being. Take some time to notice it. Wait— feel your feet on the ground. Notice your breathing in and out and in and out. Feel a rhythmical pulsating peacefulness—the oneness we already have inside us."

Dreamer paused. In that silent moment, Dreamer heard the sound of peaceful balanced horse breathing.

"How does already having peace and oneness inside you, change your experience, Talking Horse?"

Talking Horse turned around inside himself again and looked and listened and felt and waited and waited—for a signal. His tail flicked.

"A picture, an image—I don't know what changed but you are right. I can see it now. You have already rescued Precious from the clam shell and I am waiting, watching—ready to help you."

Then Talking Horse was silent, observing himself—the feelings, the pictures inside. He noticed a coming together, a remembering.

I am— I am, here, now and I always have been. I always will be. Space, I occupy—not is mine. I am peacefulness. Life is—

"Are you all right?" asked Dreamer.

"All right, and on course—of course," the horse said to Dreamer.

And then he mumbled to himself.

Yes, know— Know yes now. Now, know yes.

Dreamer was looking up, holding onto the vine. "Precious is a part of my life. I'll return with her. We have many more hallways to explore together. Even in precarious spaces, there are blossoming places For love to grow."

One tentative step at a time, Dreamer descended the vine into the unexplored cavern below. It was on the third step down that he noticed the vine no longer crackled.

It grew greener and greener and sprouted tiny green leaves and green tendrils. The golden water, the golden bath it had, seemed to nourish the vine. The main part of the live ladder swelled and grew thicker and stronger.

"The vine grows!" shouted Dreamer to Talking Horse, as he descended deeper and deeper into the cavern.

His footholds became more substantial, more secure. When Dreamer set foot on the floor of the cavern he was standing beside the clam-shell dome.

Precious was sitting there in the middle of a clam shell. Her head was down, chin dropped, almost touching her chest. Her shoulders were pulled up close to her ears. Her hands were tightly clasped, touching her clenched lips and her nose.

She was trembling. Her eyes were closed. She rocked back and forth—back and forth. She crossed her arms over her chest as if she were hugging herself.

Dreamer tapped on the dome.

It looks like she is trying to protect herself.

A startled Precious opened her eyes. She was looking into Dreamer's gentle concerned eyes.

"Am I dreaming again?"

She reached above her head and her right hand touched the dome just beneath Dreamer's hand. The dome was real.

"Are you really there?"

"Yes, I am," said Dreamer. "And I thought I heard you crying."

"I was— I was calling out to you. I thought I would never see you again."

"How did you get into that clam shell?"

Precious sighed.

"I fell into a golden lake and closed my eyes and held my breath and just when I thought I would surely die, I was sucked into a warm and transparent—comforting space. I found myself taking a deep breath of fresh air. It is a long story."

" I was following Colt. The last thing I remember before I fell into a golden lake was Cricket's faint voice saying: *See it through*."

"Cricket and the horses are waiting to see what you and Talking Horse will discover down the hallways. How did you get here?'

"Talking Horse and I followed our ears to the sound of your voice. We followed our eyes to the end of a hallway that had a golden glow. It was a dead end but it led us to the gap—the surprising entrance to this small subterranean cavern. The golden stream you came out of must flow below the central chamber."

Just then, there was a sound of escaping air—a *psssss* kind of sound and the transparent lid of the dome separated from its transparent floor. It opened a crack wide enough for Precious to roll out of the shell and she did it without thinking.

Dreamer blinked and found Precious standing beside him. He took her in his arms and hugged her.

"We must climb this ladder to the hallway above," Dreamer urged Precious. "You go first and I'll follow close behind you."

As Precious and Dreamer were climbing, the golden water receded in the rocky river banks of the cavern and the transparent dome snapped shut.

Precious looked down at the dome when she heard it snap shut. She almost lost her grip. She stopped and closed her eyes. She held her breath.

Dreamer bumped into her.

He said, "Go on! Go on. Breathe and go on."

Precious didn't move.

"Take a deep breath and go on. I don't like the look of it. The golden river's rocky banks are suddenly dry."

Still Precious didn't move.

Dreamer stepped up one more step and stood on the same step with Precious. He leaned close up against her back and put his hands on top of her hands and whispered in her ear.

"Don't look down; breathe and open your eyes and count. Take one more step. That's right—two steps, three steps."

Precious felt the reassuring warmth of Dreamer's body pressing against her. She opened her eyes and took another step up and another and another.

They were almost to the top of the braided vine ladder when they felt a wind and heard a *swoooooooosh* in the hallway.

Dreamer looked back. The small cavern was dark and the golden glow gone. It was dark now at the edge at the drop-off—at the end of the hallway.

Talking Horse asked, "What happened?"

Precious reached the top of the ledge and grabbed hold of Talking Horse's leg. Talking Horse backed up and pulled Precious out of the gap.

Dreamer swung one leg over the top of the ledge just as a rushing screaming sound filled their ears.

"Let's get out of here," said Dreamer.

They ran back down the hallway as fast as they could go in the dark. All in a sudden moment the hallway was lit up again—much brighter than it had been before.

Just as the three of them reached the central chamber, Dreamer said, "My feet are wet. It looks like the golden river is pursuing us."

Precious and Talking Horse looked back at Dreamer, leaving footprints—golden glowing footprints behind him in the hallway.

Three adventurers stopped for a few moments to look into one another's eyes and to wonder about the loud growling fury of the stream and the silent warm glow of its golden waters.

Precious said, "I'm so glad to see you two again. Thank you for rescuing me. Colt will wonder what has happened to me."

"Let's take the long way back to Storytelling Place, so Talking Horse can come with us," said Dreamer.

Talking Horse shook his head and stretched his neck and said, "Tell us what Cricket said at Storytelling Place. How did you find the golden lake?"

Dreamer interrupted Talking Horse. He had Precious by the hand. He was encouraging her.

"Don't be afraid. Turning point hallway will be dark. As we go around corners we cut off our own light from this central chamber.

Keep your hand on one wall and just keep on going. You will find Magic-Bed Tunnel. It is just a few more steps."

Talking Horse went first into the hallway. Soon the travelers were stepping onto metal tracks again. They felt a tingling vibration at their feet. There was a crash.

"The earth is not rumbling but rock is tumbling. It sounds like someone or something is moving boulders at the valley entrance to the tunnel," said Dreamer and Talking Horse almost in the same breath.

"Could it be the Sharpie?" asked Precious.

Dreamer lifted the log-brake. Precious and Dreamer pulled themselves up and over and into the boulder filled Magic Bed. Talking Horse followed Bagic bed.

Three were silent until they reached the entrance to box canyon. There, Dreamer and Precious mounted the horse.

When she felt she was on safe familiar ground again, Precious told them about her adventure at the golden lake. She was finishing her tale just as they were about to enter Storytelling Place.

"Colt may still be in the golden clearing but I'm not sure I can remember how to get there from here. I was just following Colt—not paying attention to where we were going."

Colt's mother saw Precious and Dreamer approaching on Talking Horse's back and she galloped up to them.

"She's asking, *Where's my colt*?" said Talking Horse.

"Tell her—maybe in the golden clearing."

"She says, *What golden clearing*?" said Talking Horse.

"Oh, oh, it must be a secret place—a place Colt found to get away from the herd, a place secret from even his mother, a place to be alone."

Colt's mother reared up on her hind legs and flung her front legs out as if she might like to trample Precious and when her legs hit the ground, she was still stamping one foot.

Precious was frightened. Tears came to her eyes and an uneasy feeling in her belly—right under her rib cage.

She tapped under her eye and on her chest and under her arm. More and more tears came as she began to remember the way. Precious pointed.

"There, up ahead, a faint path into the thicket—"

Suddenly Colt appeared at that very spot. He reared up on his hind legs when he saw Precious.

Then he trotted over to his mother and nuzzled her and transmitted, "How did Precious get here?"

"Precious came riding on Talking Horse's back. Just WHERE have you been all this time?"

The mother's thoughts, her transmissions, were drowned out by the sound of whinnies and the stamping of feet. Colt was distracted and looked around at all the other restless horses gathered together at Storytelling Place.

Black horses and whites, horses of all different colors were flicking their tails and anxious to hear a story about the hallways inside crystal mountain.

Cricket was resting in its niche of the fountain pedestal. The vibration of so many stamping feet jostled it and it woke.

Horse ears perked up and twitched as Cricket rubbed its legs and stretched its long antenna toward Dreamer.

"What did you discover?"

"Precious, in a dangerous cavern beneath the main cavern at the bottom of a gap at the end of a dead-end hallway—"

Dreamer paused for a moment.

"Something was guiding us. It was not just coincidence. Something shows us how to be at the right place at the exact moment we are needed."

"For Talking Horse and me, it was an inviting golden glowing hallway. We could almost feel its warming light beckoning us. When we came to a dead end, we stopped to look at one another—to contemplate."

"Then we heard it— the gurgling that enticed me to look deeper into a mysterious gap."

Precious interrupted.

"If it weren't for Talking Horse and Dreamer, I don't know where I would be, now."

Talking Horse said, "When we reached the dead end gap we heard your sobs. I can't even guess what it might be that will entice us to enter another hallway. I can't wait to see who or what we'll find there."

As if they had one mind, the restless horses scattered and left Storytelling Place to go about their daily lives and to graze deeper in the box canyon.

It was as if they already knew it would be a while before the next story—before a hallway could be found that went somewhere horse worthy.

Secret Passageways

The fountain at Storytelling Place was bubbling and the smell of fresh water was in the air. Precious and Dreamer realized for the first time, how thirsty they were. They ran to the fountain and quenched their thirst. Cricket ducked out of the way of the water and back into its niche in the fountain pedestal. Dreamer and Precious gathered fruit that had dried naturally on the vine to take with them on their coming journey.

Talking horse said, "I'll take you to the Mouth Cave of Old Stone Face, to the short way into the pink cavern and then I'll meet you at the end of Turning Point hallway."

"I'm going with you to this mysterious Turning Point and to the cavern," Colt transmitted to Talking Horse.

Talking Horse looked at Colt's mother.

She nodded her head and so he said, "Come along then, but keep your eyes and ears open."

As they galloped towards Magic Bed tunnel, Colt asked Talking Horse, "What is it like at Turning Point and inside the cavern?"

"Indescribable sights and sounds, unlike anything you have heard or seen in the box canyon or in the valley of horses. You have to have the experience. I can't tell you. Dreamer only gave you a hint about the mysteries that are there—that can be reached from the pink cavern."

Talking Horse stopped to graze and fill his belly for the coming adventure.

Colt wanted to race ahead of Talking Horse and into the tunnel. He thought he could see what was ahead of them even in the growing darkness. He was sure he could find his way but then he heard them—strange blood curdling shrieks. He shivered and remembered his mother's warnings, remembered cricket's horstories about the Sharpie.

Sun was setting behind the mountains when Dreamer and Precious climbed into Mouth Cave of Old Man in the Mountain, into what Talking Horse called Old Stone Face. They waved goodbye to Talking Horse and Colt.

Dreamer put his arm around Precious. He hugged her close to him.

She turned to face him and lifted her face to his and she seemed to melt into his body as they kissed. Their bodies pressed against one another as if they wished to be one body.

"It feels so good in your arms," said Precious.

"Precious, ohhhh Precious, you waken longings in me. I want to hold you forever."

They stood there kissing—pressed close to one another for a long while. Precious felt a kind of excitement rising in her body and yet she felt a kind of sad, empty longing again too, a feeling she couldn't quite describe, even to herself.

She was about to tell Dreamer about it when he kissed her on the forehead and said, "We had better find a place to sleep, this night before we venture into strange hallways."

Precious clung to Dreamer. She did not want to let go of him. Gently he loosened her arms and held out one hand invitingly.

Her hand went into his hand. Dreamer led her deeper into Mouth Cave.

Just a little way into the cave, Precious and Dreamer came again to the tunnel-like passage where they were forced to a crawl to continue down it. They felt their way along the tunnel walls as the light from outside began to fade away.

Dreamer's hand touched a rock that moved—that swung back into the wall of the tunnel.

"I wonder what this could be?" he said. "I didn't notice it when we passed this way before."

"What—what is it?" asked Precious.

Dreamer pushed the rock and it rolled farther back into the wall. A narrow passageway was revealed.

"It's an ascending passage way. Let's have a look."

Dreamer crawled up the dark passage way and Precious followed him to a small room. A soft light came from above.

"Look, there is an old patched robe here," said Dreamer. "And someone has carved out a reclining seat in this rock."

The seat was wide enough for two. Dreamer and Precious sat down in the seat. As they leaned back and gazed up, they saw the moon come into view through an opening in the ceiling of the room. Dreamer pulled the old robe up over them. His arm was around Precious.

She snuggled her head against his shoulder.

"This robe belongs to someone who comes here to look at the moon and the stars. I wonder who it could be."

Dreamer didn't hear her. He was already falling asleep. Precious thought she heard soft padded footsteps in the hallway as she was falling asleep.

I must remember to tell Dreamer.

As Talking Horse and Colt stopped to graze, evening fell and a full moon rose to light their way. Colt was anxious to go on to Turning Point and the mysterious cavern inside the mountain.

"There is no hurry," said Talking Horse. "Precious and Dreamer will be sleeping now. We'll meet them at the cavern, tomorrow."

Oh please, please—let's go on to turning point.

He couldn't have said it any plainer if he had used words. Colt would not stop prancing and coaxing and throwing his head, so Talking Horse gave in and led Colt into Magic Bed tunnel.

Inside they found the dark, side-passageway, because Talking Horse knew it was there and not because they could see in the dark.

They felt their way—bumping noses and ears against the rough sides of the passageway. Finally, they could see a pink glow from the central cavern.

Talking Horse said, "We'll wait in the hallway, when we get to the cavern, so Precious and Dreamer can find us. Don't enter the central crystal cavern till morning."

Colt wasn't paying attention to Talking Horse. He was so excited by the enticing light he saw in front of him he bolted into the cavern. Then he stopped and blinked his eyes at the strange sights and sounds.

Crystal pillars and pink light, everywhere light from gold, pink, white, green crystals—

Colt's tail was swishing and a faint musical swish echoed in the chamber. Talking Horse nosed Colt and nudged him back into the passageway.

"You heard the music," he said. "Every sound is echoed and reechoed in this chamber, even our footsteps. It is best to be as silent as you can be crossing the threshold."

Excitement danced inside Colt and he pranced and pranced in Turning Point hallway. He saw so many more hallways he wanted to explore. He dashed past Talking Horse into the pink chamber.

Talking Horse watched Colt turn to the left and start down the next closest hallway. Talking Horse lifted off his front legs and stamped back down again. He Shook his head, swished his tail and twitched his ears as he ran after Colt.

Suddenly, as he was crossing the threshold to the next hallway, there was an ominous rumbling sound. Talking Horse, stopped, looked around and finally looked up just in time to get out of the way of a strange wall that was descending.

The wall nearly hit Talking Horse on his hind quarters. Talking Horse reared up on his hind quarters again and whinnied and stamped his feet until Colt looked back at him.

"Now just look at what you have done."

Talking Horse turned around in the hallway and nosed the transparent wall blocking their way back into the cavern.

"We can't get back into the main cavern."

Colt could still see the cavern and thought Talking Horse must be losing his senses.

"*Oh, yes we can,*" Colt transmitted.

He turned around—ran past Talking Horse and right into the transparent wall.

Colt shook his head and stretched his neck and let out a sad whinny. Talking Horse was not one bit sympathetic.

"We must stand here by this strange wall until morning, Colt. You had better shape up and hope that Dreamer and Precious can find us. They will have to find a way to release us."

Colt hung his head down. He and Talking Horse stood at the transparent wall, staring into the pink cavern. Finally they closed their eyes.

There was only the sound of horse breathing in the hallway. Colt was almost asleep when he heard something other than horse breathing. He had never heard such a sound before. He opened one eye.

Something furry white—slinking in the cavern, crossing the hallway— no, it couldn't be. Such an animal has never been seen. Couldn't be here. I have just been dreaming.

Colt's eyelid was heavy, so heavy.

Morning will come faster if I sleep. No need to stay awake.

His eye closed and he fell into a deep sleep.

Wizard's Work

Again and again, something drew the Sharpie, that monstrous black bird with the murderous talons, back to the door. The door was still open. The Sharpie jerked the metal ring again and then stomped with both feet on the opened door. She heard Talking Horse and Dreamer working inside the tunnel.

I will have what's inside—

She scratched and dug and rolled one boulder out of the tunnel but her foot was too big to reach other deeper boulders and small rocks blocking her way. She bent her head down and put one eye up to the cavity.

What is at the other end of this tunnel? Voices I hear, voices. I see a little light. Whatever is inside uses this doorway. A door and a doorway to—

Suddenly the Sharpie stamped its foot again.

Who uses the door? I don't have to wait till they come out. I'll crack a hole in this mountain.

The monstrous bird lifted one foot and stomped as hard as she could against the open doorway but the tunnel stayed intact. She was discouraged for the moment.

She flapped her wings and lifted into the air. She looked back over her shoulder as she flew to her cave. She was snorting and shaking her foot when she landed on her own ledge. Suddenly something caught her attention.

"Movement—there's movement at the back of the cave."

She was about to rush in—to attack but her foot sank into something on the ledge and it released an irresistible aroma.

Food— it smells so good and I am hungry.

Her talons tore into it—the silver something so conveniently waiting for her.

What is this? And it's not gold but silver? Hungry! Strange! It tastes good this time.

She cocked her head and hesitated.

Now, why do I think—this time?

She gulped more of the silver food. Her belly was full but she was not satisfied. *"AASCHHEEIIM"*

How did it get here?

Wondering increased her appetite again. She continued to gorge, until she was stuffed—full up to the craw. Only then did the Sharpie settle down on her claws and ruffle her tail feathers—to rest and to ponder.

Food, all this food ready and waiting for me—not bitter, this time. Why do I keep thinking, this time?

The Sharpie's head drooped and her thoughts slowed. She was falling into a kind of stupor. Sleep was beckoning her.

I must re—member.

When the black bird opened its eyes the next morning, everything seemed to be larger.

The cave—I don't remember the cave being so far above my head.

She sat on the ledge of her cave for a few minutes but then she was drawn to the sound again. She lifted black iridescent wings and flew down the mountainside. She flew right by the metal ring and past the open door into the mountainside.

She perched on a boulder inside Magic Bed tunnel and walked sideways over to a crevice between the boulders. She stuck her head thru the boulders and then wiggled her shoulders until she was standing on the other side of the cave-in.

She crow-hopped, onto a boulder and then flapped her wings and flew down the tunnel to Turning Point. She looked back at the space she had come thru.

"Caw—caw caw caw," she screamed over and over again.

Caw! Caw! Caw! woke Precious and Dreamer. Dreamer cocked his head.

"Did you hear that? It sounds like a crow and I didn't know there were any crows in this valley."

"That reminds me; I heard a sound like padded footsteps as we fell asleep last night."

Dreamer shook his head.

"I wonder what prowls at night. Lucky we found this room when we did. We slept safe from whatever it is that prowls this cavern."

"I hope Talking Horse and Colt are safe," said Precious.

Dreamer crawled down the descending passageway to the rolling rock. As he pushed it away he cautiously poked his head out into Mouth Cave hallway and then he motioned for Precious to follow him.

They stood side by side for a few minutes at the entrance to the pink cavern. They stared at Turning Point hallway. Talking Horse and Colt were not there.

Precious put her arm around Dreamer's waist and laid her head on his shoulder and whispered, "I'm afraid for Talking Horse and Colt."

Cautiously the two explorers walked hand in hand toward Turning Point hallway. Their footsteps echoed but Precious thought she heard a faint whinny.

She pointed to the next hallway and to her ear. She put her finger to her lips. They were tiptoeing.

All at once they saw Talking Horse and Colt standing part way down the next hallway.

Precious ran to greet them. She was so excited and glad to see Talking Horse and Colt, she didn't even pause to wonder why they just stood there— why they didn't come to greet her.

Precious didn't watch where she was going and bumped right into the almost invisible barrier. There was a major rumbling and then the hallway shook.

The Wizard was retreating at the back of the cave just as the Sharpie landed on the ledge and found the food he had prepared for her. He froze in his tracks so his movements wouldn't attract the Sharpie.

When he was sure she was occupied with eating and wasn't coming after him, he turned around and slipped into the crack at the back of the cave. It was just wide enough to allow him to enter the Sharpie's cave and narrow enough to keep her on her side of the crack.

He tiptoed up a "Y" shaped narrow passageway. His cave was above the Sharpie's cave and at the end of the short perpendicular part of the "Y"— at the place of junction to the other two passageways.

The Wizard rolled a concealing rock across the back entrance to his cave. Still he couldn't avoid hearing the Sharpie tearing into its food.

In the fading evening light, he unrolled again, the piece of a scroll he found stashed in a crevice in the left side of the "Y". There was a pile of silver dust under it.

Who could have put it there in that dead end hallway? Had someone been excavating—mining for silver there?

He muttered to himself.

Fragment, not everything, not a whole scroll—

He read again the rhymed recipe.

When what is gold is turned to silver, a cruel giant shrinks. It will not behold the change unless by chance it stops and drinks and sees it own reflection, unless by chance it—

The scroll was torn at that very place and how much was unsaid, how much was unread, a Wizard didn't know. Suddenly he was so tired he thought he couldn't take another step.

I can't imagine why I am so tired. Must lie down.

He didn't remember his Herculean struggle— dragging the goat onto the ledge. It was a few minutes before he fell asleep. A thought kept flickering, almost kept him awake.

It was such a coincidence that I should find a dead golden goat and this pile of silver dust near my cave.

Finally he leaned back and closed his eyes. As he was falling asleep, he revisited what he thought was his last night's dream.

Odd dream—I thought I struck a hanging crystal with a crystal wand. And then there were musical multi-tones. I was tingling, stretching, growing. Warm, warmer— I tried to remove my robe. Oh, no— I was wearing a white fur coat underneath my robe and I couldn't take it off. My feet, my feet were light as panther feet.

Inside his dream, a huge white panther raced out of the central chamber and bounded back up the hallway to the cave above the Sharpie's cave—to the Wizard's cave. The wizard wasn't there. The cat sat down on his haunches and lifted his nose in the air.

Goat scent! Yes! A golden mountain goat!

Stalking, silent, panther feet were slinking down the mountain path to the parting of three ways. A goat stood beside a black rock.

In one giant leap, the panther landed with all four feet on the back of the goat. It sank its teeth into the goat's neck. It was done quickly.

The big cat dragged the goat closer to the Wizard's cave and then dropped it. It entered the cave and paced back and forth, back and forth as if it were waiting for someone to appear.

A slight growl escaped from its throat as it left the cave and stepped onto the path to the valley again. It traveled across a faint crack in the path where, near-by, there was a black standing stone.

At the black stone, the panther paused, pulled in its claws and licked its paws and then cleaned its face and whiskers. Just a faint taste of the adventure remained but the taste of it was exciting.

The panther sat down on its haunches and felt the warm wind caress its whiskers. It was thirsty. A long white tail swished and ears turned, ever so slightly to catch the sound. And then it was bounding along a river and toward water erupting from the side of the mountain.

Roaring tumbling water created a fog like spray and in the sunlight. A rainbow— The cat curled one big front paw and tried to snatch the rainbow from the fog. In one great leap it was standing on a ledge just behind the waterfall. It drank from a cup shaped indentation on the ledge and entered a dark cool place in the side of the mountain.

It was stretching out and lying down on the cool floor of the cave—staring at the waterfall from inside waterfall cave. Suddenly a surge of wild enthusiasm moved it.

I have the legs for it. I'll find the source of this waterfall.

Just above this cave, water was running over a red rock ledge and gushing from a crack in the mountain.

The panther crouched and lunged for the ledge and dug its toe-nails in. It was slipping, barely hanging on—almost falling off the side of the mountain and it left white scratch marks in the wet red rock.

Finally a wet panther pulled itself up and onto the red rock ledge, took a few steps and poked its nose down into the cracked rock that spilled water.

Another narrow ledge, a path inside—

The rocks brushed its whiskers. It would be a tight squeeze. A roar came out of the panther's mouth as it built up courage to drop down onto the path.

The river divides—two different flows, one flow to the right beside the path. Traces of a golden color in the water disappear into a crack. The splash sounds hollow. Is there a cavern below?

The other flow, colorless—where does it go? Get a better look on the ledge above my head?

It came to the end of the passageway where there was only a deep crack in the wall of rock.

Barely enough room—

It wiggled and squeezed thru it on its belly and then it could see.

Familiar—the pink glowing light and crystal chamber, golden hallway off to one side—

Hidden—the golden river flowing underground there—

It had broken through to one of the corridors that seemed to go on and on deeper into the mountain. Finally, it could stand up, on all four feet again. It was licking its coat, cleaning its belly when panther cat eyes saw it just slightly ahead.

A *Beam of blue light, belly high—*

It crossed the beam, interrupted its light and continued down the hallway. There was a deep rumbling in the passageway and a transparent barrier was lifted. The cat's ears were twitching.

Something invites me to go on.

It sauntered on deeper and deeper into the mountain. Its faint growl sounded like—Ooonnemmuugggh.

It turned its head from side to side, stopped for a minute to rub its ears with one paw and then another. Then it sat on its haunches and sniffed the air.

The scent of another animal.

Padded silent feet were prowling inside the mountain.

Something here for a cat like me.

When the Wizard woke from his nap and his dream, he was puzzled and not refreshed. He was tired, so very tired but he couldn't help thinking.

"There is something here for a cat like me."

He listened for the Sharpie again but didn't hear its heavy feet stomping and didn't hear its huge wings rustling. He descended the short, narrow passageway between caves.

It was a few minutes before sunrise. There was another crack between the caves where he could peek at her. It was too narrow for the Sharpie to squeeze her claws through but he had to be on the lookout. One sharp talon might still reach for him if the Sharpie suspected he was there.

First rays of morning light were brightening even the far recesses of the Sharpie's cave. He knew he was vulnerable but he had to see for himself. A slight movement caught the Wizard's eye.

A bird flew from the ledge of the Sharpie's cave—a small ordinary black bird.

Not a sign of the Sharpie anywhere.

The Wizard ventured out into the cave and then onto the ledge of the Sharpie's cave. He searched the sky for the Sharpie. He watched the small, bird as it flew, around and around in circles—diving down, down towards the path on the mountain.

It was flying to the metal ring. No, past the metal ring and then into the opened doorway in the side of the mountain.

Exactly what the Sharpie would do. Hooray, the ancient shrinking formula works but for how long? The missing piece of scroll—I must find it.

Invisible Barriers

Precious thudded right into something she couldn't see and stumbled backwards. Dreamer caught her in his arms and held her tenderly against him. He kissed her nose.

"Did you hurt yourself?"

They saw their own images reflected in what was blocking the way just before the weighty something lifted.

There was a rumbling and flashes of light. Talking Horse and Colt were freed. They pranced out into the end of the hallway as if it were an everyday occurrence to be caught behind invisible barriers.

"What? When? How? Who opens it up? I thought you were supposed to meet us at Turning Point hallway."

"You're right, Dreamer. I— that is— we knew that. It's a bit of a story that turns out all right."

"Colt was impetuous and wanted to see the sights and we were caught behind this—this invisibleness until you released us. Oh yes, one thing more—it might be important. Colt told me, that just before he fell asleep he saw something white cross the hallway entrance."

Dreamer nodded.

"Precious heard soft padded footsteps where we slept. It was probably a bit of good luck that you were behind that invisible door last night. Something does prowl the cavern."

Before the adventurers entered the main cavern again they heard and then felt another rumble. They didn't see what was descending in the distance or what was approaching them from the far end of that passageway.

Colt's ears were twitching and he was swinging his head and almost prancing in place.

"We can explore four ways, all at once if we each take a corridor."

Talking Horse shook his head.

"Colt wants to explore on his own."

Dreamer looked at Colt.

"No, a colt needs a little guidance. I'll go with him. You go with Precious and we'll tackle two corridors at once. Meet you here at Invisible-Door hallway. Take care of Precious."

The Eagle

The Wizard didn't remember returning to his cave. It seemed to him that the cave conspired to jostle him, to wake him and he was still so tired, so very tired. He reached for his bottle of Ynnaline.

Just brush one drop on my tongue— Need some energy, some refreshment—

One drop of the bitter liquid touched his tongue and then an eagle soared from the ledge of the Wizard's cave and circled and soared down the mountainside to a waterfall.

The eagle folded its wings and then stepped into the waterfall and through the thundering water to a warm dry cave at the base of the mountain. The great bird shook its wings and sat at the mouth of the cave as if it were dazed—just staring at the waterfall. The sound of thundering water lulled it to sleep.

The Wizard was rubbing his eyes.

I must have fallen asleep. I don't remember coming to this place. How? How can I be at Waterfall Cave?

He was stroking his long white beard.

I'm cold—and wet! I must get my robe.

He started down a corridor at the back of the cave. The door was already open. He stepped over a blue beam and then he reached over his head and broke another blue beam. The door descended behind him and sealed the back end of the cave and the entrance to the hallway.

It's good to be safe from intruders.

He walked half-way down the hallway and raised his hand and broke another beam. An invisible barrier in front of him was lifted and a few moments later, he walked out into the pink glow.

He turned right, at the next hallway. Soon he was crawling down the hallway. He pushed on the wall and a rock rolled back. He entered an ascending passageway to a cozy little room.

Sun was shining through an opening in the ceiling of the room. His robe was draped across a reclining rock seat. He sat down and was warmed by the sun as he pulled on his robe. The Wizard's eyes grew heavy.

He slept until a faint, *Caw* , finally woke him. He pulled the rock back and listened.

There was no one there with him but still he said out loud, "I *must* see to that bird."

The Wizard left his safe and cozy place of observation behind him and descended into the cramped connecting passage way he would have to negotiate.

He looked into the soft light at Storytelling Place and back at the pink glow from the central chamber. Slowly the Wizard crawled to the place where he could stand up in Mouth-Cave at Old Stone Face of Man in the Mountain. He heard it again—Caw, caw.

Caw Caw

The black bird didn't stop to turn at Turning Point but flew on to the light at the end of magic-bed tunnel.

Ahaa, caw— from this secret passageway, I can sneak up on them.

The bird spied a young colt and tried to cackle its delight but just *Caw Caw* came out of its mouth.

It tried to grab the colt's rump but its foot just didn't reach around a colt anymore. The bird crash landed on the back of that small grazing colt.

The startled youngster kicked its hind legs and sent the bird flying off screaming.

"Caw, awwwk—CAW!"

A furious, black bird flew around and around in big circles screaming, scolding the herd of horses. The horses weren't paying any attention. Finally the bird tired and flew off toward the thicket to find a place to perch.

It looked around at the horses and huffed and puffed up its chest and closed its eyes to scream at them one last time. The bird was flying in a blind rage and banged right into a branch.

When it opened its eyes again it was lying on its back on the horse path that led to Storytelling Place. The bird strained and struggled to roll over and finally it was able to pick itself up. It stood there ruffling chest feathers and stretching out wings. But it was so dizzy, it staggered and hopped around and when it finally sat down on its tail feathers, it was stunned into silence with what it found.

Clearing— Fountain!

It sat there for a few minutes blinking its eyes, staring at the fountain. When it took to the air again it flew to the fountain and perched there on top of the pedestal looking around at the bramble and thicket enclosed space—a place it had not seen before.

Stone head on the side of the mountain, wizard standing there in its mouth— I remember a Wizard—something about a Wizard. What is it?

The Wizard made some strange passes with his hands that drew the bird to him. It flew to Mouth-Cave and sat at his feet.

"Come along with me."

The Wizard was patting his shoulder.

"I'll find you something good to eat."

As the bird was flying to his shoulder it spotted something caught in a crevice in the roof of mouth cave. It couldn't resist pulling it out. The Wizard looked up.

"What have you found?"

The bird perched on his shoulder was toying with a torn piece of a narrow scroll. It was reluctant to give up what it held in its beak.

The Wizard raised his hand, closed his fingers and waved his open palm in front of the bird's right eye. He made a horizontal pass, another slanted pass straight down and then slow, continuous circular motions of his hand.

The bird was fascinated, forgot about its treasure. With thumb and first finger of his left hand, Onemug gently grasped the scroll.

The bird noticed the tug, opened its mouth to protest but then lost its grip. Now the suspicious crow was watching his every movement. Stomping on his shoulder.

Can't believe I lost it.

The Wizard was speaking softly, slowly, varying his tone of voice.

"You can *relax*. It is all right to *let it go*. It's in my hand *now*. It was too *heavy for you*, too hard to do—the holding on."

Black crow eyes were following his hand motions.

"Your eyes are tired. You have been so tense. You want to feel better. It feels so good to *relax. Lids heavy— so heavy you want to settle down and rest now."*

The Wizard's voice was sometimes bold and assertive and sometimes as intimate as a whisper. The bird's eyes were blinking. It's head was drooping. It was settling down on his shoulder—staring and blinking.

The Wizard made some passes with his hands—one that looked like a slanted "L" and another like the figure "5" connecting to it. He encompassed the whole figure in an elongated semi-circle and then he added two small semi-circles to the stretched semi-circle.

The bird's head followed his motions. The crow began to sway. There were some kind of pulsations in its feet—rising to its chest, to its heart. It cocked its head to hear what Onemug was saying.

"It is so comfortable for you to learn something new. There is an *unconscious* part of you that can *integrate conscious and unconscious parts—encourage resourceful parts to take pleasure landing* on the right place at the right time *to be* successful."

The Wizard was speaking in many different tones again—almost as if he were speaking to different beings.

"You feel *the breeze* lifting *the feathers of your wings. Your* body *feels heavy. Your feet are grasping*—resting *on a soft shoulder."*

The bird opened its mouth and was panting.

"You are aware of the tongue *in your mouth*. You feel *the air pass over it as you take a deep breath. You* have found a *safe and comfortable place to* perch."

The bird was sleepy and so comfortable—so relaxed. She closed her mouth and without even one protesting caw she tucked her head under a wing and prepared to nap.

The Wizard was silent, nodding his head to the rhythm of the bird's breathing. He was rubbing his hands, palms together in a circular motion that joined in the rhythm of her eye movements under closed lids.

He whispered again.

"*You have learned something very interesting.* You will wake refreshed . You will *continue to learn*—head tucked under a wing, eyes closed. It is *so comfortable learning this way—resting* your feet on my shoulder. Sleep now and have *peaceful* dreams until I wake you. Thank you. It is done."

The black bird fell into a deep sleep and dreamed she was searching for and finding pieces of something magical. She was gathering the pieces, putting them together like a jig-saw puzzle. A picture was beginning to take shape.

Something Missing

Colt's mother was uneasy.

"Why did I agree to let Colt enter that strange place deep inside Possibility Mountain—that space we have all been avoiding?"

She kept returning to Storytelling Place to look into Mouth-Cave and then she galloped from Storytelling Place to the entrance at Magic-Bed tunnel. Back and forth she ran looking for some sign of the explorers.

Today she was resting at Storytelling Place. She shook her mane and out of the corner of her eye she noticed a slight movement in Mouth-Cave. She looked up at the Wizard speaking to a black bird on his shoulder.

The Wizard looked directly at Colt's mother and motioned for her to come to him. Something about his hands were entrancing to her.

Every time she took a step, he moved a hand. Every time she threw her head from side to side, he moved a hand in the same rhythm. She was drawn to do his bidding, to stand with her flank up against the mountain, beneath mouth cave.

"Thank you," said the Wizard as he stepped onto her back and then onto the sacred storytelling ground. "It is done."

He held up the crow's fortuitous find, the scraggly rolled up piece of scroll. In the light at Storytelling Place he could read what was written on it.

Watering the soul awakens a seed and uncovers the need.

The Wizard whispered again to the crow.

" Wake, *you must be hungry. Drink*, eat slowly, without haste. *Forget the former bitter taste. Take one bite* so sweet you are *satisfied.* I cannot be denied. *Return to me, to rest, to sleep again.*"

A docile black bird flew from the Wizard's shoulder and drank from the fountain at Storytelling Place. She ate some tart fruit. After one bite of sweet fruit, she returned to the Wizard's shoulder and folded her wings.

Colt's mother was watching the bird and the Wizard with some suspicion. The Wizard was unrolling a fragile fragment of scroll. He was reading.

You touch the sacred core once more. The fountain inside you quenches a thirst but first, satisfy a hunger, taste heart-shaped fruit— wearing a different suit.

At this point in the scroll not only a few words but whole lines were missing.

When three become one,
brutal, clawing, screaming is done
———————————

beyond heavy blocking boulders
———————————

a Wizard's shoulders————

The Wizard shook his head yes. It looked like there might be a clue to what was still in store for him and the bird. As he unrolled the scroll he was astounded at what came next. Nothing but empty space and finally a lonesome word.

———————— *gravity—*

His mouth dropped open and he muttered.

"There has to be more to it. Not so much as a brush stroke mars the space around it. Gravity commands my attention. What don't I see?"

He was determined to unroll the narrow scroll to its very end and there it was again— *Gravity* beginning another sentence. He began to read.

Gravity and time, dawn at sunset— ride the event horizon. Know a dark attractor spinning time. What abides in gravity, glides into the humorous core. Seek and find a new clear vision (not nuclear fission.) More powerful, beneficent, energy fields known long ago, wait for you to use them. A blue pearl swirls at the edge of a milky stream riding the waves of a formidable, fomenting black sea. The gem will be polished in time to take her appointed place in the heavenly necklace of space. Be aware of her new direction heading to a re-connection. The whole, conscious mind—call-o-sum— unites a re-membering cosmic body-mind, arms and legs— the mirror, the great cosmic work. Holographic invitations go out. A scattered flock gathers————The Conference of Birds.

There were no more words. The Wizard muttered.

"What Conference of Birds?"

As he rolled up the scroll, he was talking to himself.

"Shouldn't— it— be——— Conference of Words?"

Colt's mother was shaking her head, stamping one foot, twitching her ears, keeping one eye on the Wizard.

How did that Wizard? What was I doing letting him step on my back, like that? It has been too long. Something must have happened to Colt.

She galloped back to Magic-Bed tunnel entrance and followed the metal tracks.

I must see for myself what dangers Colt faced.

The earth trembled. Rocks dropped on the tracks.

Why did I let him go? How could I let him go out of my sight?

She kept on going but her head was hanging down and her footsteps were plodding.

What if— what if—

She remembered her grandmother's advice.

Go thru it or stand your ground. When fear blows over you, you can find ways around it or through it. It's no more substantial than a stinky piff—flatulence, the undigested making itself known. Walk away from stinking thinking. Find your answers somewhere tails are swishing—where sweet breezes blow, where grass can grow tall and green. The peaceful somewhere air smells fragrant and clean.

It was her grandmother's urging that kept her going, today. *Trot girl, trot!—* She could almost hear it. She lifted her head and trotted on. At Turning Point she didn't hesitate—turned down the dark tunnel.

She bumped and scraped her ears and nose, in a frightening emptiness and darkness she had not known before. Finally, a waft of fresh air, sweet as the fruit at Storytelling Place, reached her nose. She could almost hear her grandmother's whinny.

Did she know? Did she visit this place?

Colt's mother rounded a corner and stepped into light that was blinding at first. Blinking back tears, she stood on the threshold of pink and gold and so many other beautiful colors.

By my grandmother— What is happening? Will I ever see my Colt again?

Finally her eyes adapted to the strange light. She was staring into the circular central cavern and hallways going off in every direction.

Colt's mother caught her breath and held it as what came into focus was a white panther taking a step, hesitating, taking another step.

What does it stalk? Something down that hallway. I must follow it in case it stalks Colt.

Learning To Communicate

As Precious and Talking Horse explored deeper into the hallway, the hallway was losing its light.

"Why aren't you talking to me? Why don't you say something?" Precious asked Talking Horse.

Talking horse looked back at her.

"Now I just am. I explore the quiet way."

"But, you are called, Talking Horse."

"Yes, YES, that is because I can talk when I choose to talk, that is—WHEN, I have something to say to you."

There was a tone of irritation in his voice. The horse stopped walking and stood still.

"Listen! Something may be sneaking up on us."

Precious leaned forward.

"What do you mean? Have you heard something?"

"Sshhhhhhhhhh, I can't hear anything but your voice. For goodness sakes— Shhhhhhhh!"

Precious was quiet for only a few moments.

"It is sound that is comforting to me. The tone of your voice, strong and confident like my father's voice is like music to my ears—

especially when I can't see where we are. I don't like your dark silences. I even long to hear your comforting clip clops now."

Talking Horse lifted his head up and stretched his neck and tried to look her in the eye.

"*I feel* what you are not hearing. While you, while we are conversing—the ground under us is changing.

"Are you sure? How do you know?"

Talking Horse stopped and tested the ground.

"Too dark to see but *it feels* spongy underfoot."

"Do I hear you saying, you don't know what we might be stepping into?" asked Precious.

Talking horse stopped in his tracks and looked over his shoulder at Precious again.

"You do have noisy thoughts in the dark."

She said, "I'm depending on you. What if you get stuck?"

Talking Horse turned around and headed back to the central chamber at the very same instant Precious heard an inner voice.

Turn around; go back to the light—to the music.

Talking horse said, "Sounds are important to you; aren't they? It's *hearing* words that ring your bell."

Precious shook her head.

"Yes, you are clear as a bell. And *feeling* words, *action* words hit the mark for you. You hear— oops I should say, you grasp my meaning better when I use feeling words or action words."

They were learning to communicate better when they both caught a glimpse of something white crossing their pathway at crystal cavern.

Colt was frisky, prancing faster and faster down the hallway. Dreamer was enjoying the romp, was not restraining—not urging the colt to slow down. Colt and Dreamer had a kind of rapport that allowed Colt to transmit his thoughts and that allowed Dreamer to understand them—to respond to them. Dreamer and Colt rode as one— breathing together, sharing one another's thoughts.

When they came to a sharp turn in the hallway, they lost light from the central chamber but there was soft light and a glow ahead. It seemed to be hovering above the ground and hugging the sides of the hallway. It was faint but enough to see by and so they went on.

Colt turned his head to one side and looked back at Dreamer.

"You look old to me. Are you old?"

"No—yes, I suppose, you might consider me old although I don't feel old inside myself. I feel as young as a colt."

Colt stamped his feet.

"Are you going to be like the elders who are always trying to hold me back?"

Dreamer patted Colt's neck.

"I might look like an elder to you but I know the feeling—the longing to go fast and free. You may be misunderstanding elders."

Colt reared up.

Dreamer shook his head.

"Is it *holding you back* if someone asks, do you know where your next mouthful of hay will come from? Do you know where you will sleep? Do you know the road?"

"Elders know from experience that you might need a clue about what might be ahead of you—like a washout of the road now and again."

Dreamer patted Colt on the neck again.

"If you think an elder is holding you back, it may be you are recognizing some part of yourself that you have ignored, that you don't want to see."

Colt snorted.

"I can't hold myself back."

"Yes, yes you can. We all learn how and when to do it. Sooner or later we all come up against a relationship that is difficult for us. Welcome that experience. It brings a gift to you. Dealing with or walking away from a relationship we can learn about our strengths and our weaknesses."

"Eventually we learn who problems belong to. Knowing yourself is important. It helps you succeed. When you know yourself, you will know that if you don't get what you want something better than you ever dreamed of is waiting for you."

"Life events wait for you to catch up to them. When you are ready for pleasant surprises—you find them."

"What do you mean by that?"

"You know—I mean Colt, you can find the patience, the peacefulness at your core. Taming the fearful parts of you, lets you get on with succeeding and completing your whole life story."

Enchantment

Colt snorted again.

"How do you know? How many whole life stories do you know?"

"A few. Talking Horse told me about some of the washouts on his road."

Colt reared up a little.

"When he was a colt?"

"He wasn't a colt. It's time you heard his story. This is what he told me."

My father was king. I had the best of everything—the finest clothes. I was a prince. When it was time for my schooling, teachers from near and far came to the king's court to apply for the royal job of mentor to the prince. My father chose a silken tongued, bearded teacher in a long robe.

He became a fixture of the royal court. Perhaps in some strange way he still teaches me today about deception. He was an evil Ginn (in teacher disguise) or a teacher (in evil Ginn disguise. Whatever—

The silken tongued one was wily and pretended a knowledge of herbs. He gained the king's confidence and offered him an intoxicating elixir that would take all his troubles away.

More often than not at court banquets, the Ginn sat beside my father and offered him an entrancing potion. My father was changed so much I didn't recognize him as my father anymore and I just called him, *the king.*

The King enjoyed the Ginn's brew and didn't care or didn't seem to notice that when he drank the brew his words slurred. The wily one laughed and told the King that he was being funny—that he had an infectious sense of humor.

The courtiers were concerned and intimidated by the king and at the Ginn's suggestion they laughed half-heartedly and nervously. I didn't laugh. There was nothing to laugh about.

Soon, if anyone spoke one word against the teacher-Ginn, the king raged. The King was lashing out at his most loyal advisers. It was happening over and over again. When the King wasn't under the influence of the Ginn's so called tonic, he felt more and more alone and so the King decreed that the bearded one and his elixir should never leave his side.

One day the imposter sat beside the King and grew bold enough to propose a toast.

The King and I agree the prince is special and shall not be like anyone else in this kingdom. He is tutored by a Ginn—ius—

He almost made a mistake and called himself by name. The Ginn planned a coup.

The prince must taste the King's elixir.

He leaned over to whisper a spell in my Princely ear.

From time to time you are a talking horse, because of course, the King is hoarse and not himself. He is just aha ha ha ha—bound to be much worse for his drunken blaring and you shall be wearing his horse's tail along with an undecipherable whinny. That's what you will inherit from him and I shall inherit the kingdom.

From now on if you try to tell the King about himself or about me your voice will whinny. No one else dares to tell him about himself, or about his beloved Ginn and so—I win

I heard what the Ginn said but I didn't believe it. I begged my father to listen. I thought I could tell him about the Ginn but he wouldn't—maybe he couldn't hear me. My pleading did sound more and more like whinnies.

When I tried to talk to my father, the Ginn's voice almost hissed at me.

The kingdom is mine. No one stops me from pinning a tail to the prince of this kingdom.

"No! It is not so, I screamed at the Ginn, my father would never allow it. A King will not stay under the influence of a Ginn, forever."

The King's eyes didn't see me. I tried to grab the bottle away from the King. He was still holding the bottle in his hand, even though his head was nodding, nodding.

He fell forward and fast asleep at the banquet table. Before I could grab the bottle the Ginn snatched it from the King's hand and laughed at me.

He threw his head back and gave a loud belly laugh. He inflated himself to his most ominous size and he began to cast his evil spells over the subjects of the kingdom.

You do not see me. And of course, if a prince says, "Free Me," you will see a horse.

No one dared to stand up to the Ginn or to even look him in the eyes. Then the evil Ginn turned his attention to me.

A prince must taste what a King tastes. Drink, you'll be like your father. I'll see to it.

I didn't really resist because I was curious about the elixir and I thought a few sips couldn't harm me. I thought.

I know and I see what is going on and so the Ginn will not influence me.

I drank from the Ginn's bottle but I whispered to some part of myself.

Let there be some good that comes from this experience.

The Ginn was laughing.

You will become a horse-prince now just like your father.

He tilted the bottle and I almost choked on the liquid that was now burning my throat. I tried to spit it out but the Ginn held my nose until I swallowed it all.

I staggered. I screamed when I could breathe again. It sounded more like a horrible whinny. The only thing that kept me from throwing myself off a cliff was my grandmother's stories. Her words came back to me.

True love can provide protection against any evil spell.

I whinnied and wondered if a horse-prince could or would ever find true love.

The Ginn stayed close to me—began to influence my thoughts and tried to discourage me. He began to deepen his spell.

You royal highness horse, will obey me, even after you marry. Your wife will see you sometimes as a prince and sometimes as a horse. Of course, you must tell her to keep your secret.

(There will be drastic consequences for you if she tells anyone else in the kingdom about your transformations.)

But, you may not tell her about that part of your enchantment. Do not try to warn her. If you try to warn her, you will lose your voice. It will become a whinny. Eventually the kingdom will be mine because no one will stop me in time.

The Ginn was so gleeful he let it slip how the spell might be removed.

No one will call me by name and so it is decreed by a Ginn.

I heard him chuckling to himself.

She won't know the consequences. His wife won't keep the secret. He will have to abdicate his inheritance and I will occupy the throne.

The Ginn doubled over in a fit of laughter all the while growing bigger and more demanding with every drop he poured down my throat at the King's banquets.

The King continued to sleep at his own banquet table. No one mentioned my condition, or his. One by one the court tiptoed out of the room—wise men, ministers, even the jesters.

Finally, one day I clopped out of the banquet hall to get a breath of fresh air. I was feeling four feet on the ground, was tasting grass in a velvety soft mouth. My own tail was swishing.

Dreamer patted Colt's neck.

"I remember tears streaking down Talking Horse's face. There was no need to tell me more."

"Tell me more," said Colt. "Will Talking Horse find someone to name the Ginn—to speak the unspeakable undoing magic for him?"

Dreamer thought Colt could do some thinking on his own.

"Don't you know? Can't you guess? Aren't we nearing the end of his story?"

Colt and Dreamer fell into a kind of reverie— contemplating how Talking Horse's story might end. A flash of light and their own reflections stopped them, just in time to avoid a crash into an unfamiliar barrier.

" What? What is it?"

Precious and Talking Horse returned to the central cavern. Colt's mother was at the end of magic-bed hallway. She was staring at the hallway Colt and Dreamer had gone down. Precious waved to Colt's mother.

Talking Horse said, "She says she saw the tail end of a slinky white panther entering that hallway. Somehow she already knows her colt has gone down that hallway and she is frozen with fear—afraid to take one step— not knowing how to help him."

"Tell her to come with us. We'll go down the hallway together and together we'll meet up with whatever we meet up with," said Precious.

She motioned—*come on*— to Colt's mother.

Talking Horse whispered.

"Come with us."

Crystals verberated and reverberated.

Come with us—with us—with us—come.

Colt's mother clopped with heavy hoofs into the crystal chamber.

Clip, clop—clip, clop——clop—

Crystals sang to her every footstep.

Carol C. McFall

Talking Horse was stepping gingerly, quietly and whispering.

"Too much sound—too much, too much is disorienting."

The travelers were not far into the soft glow in Panther Hallway when they heard Dreamer exclaiming.

"Look! Colt, the Wizard and a crow and something or someone coming up the hallway behind them."

When Colt's mother heard Dreamer say *Colt* she bolted ahead and nosed right into her own colt. She ignored the others who were just staring at one another.

She leaned her neck against her colt's neck and sent her thoughts to him.

So much to tell you.

Story for a Colt

Danger! White panther! Afraid for you! I might not always be here. You don't know some of our horsestories—ones you might need to know.

My mother, your grandmother was good at swishing up a tale especially when I needed it. I must tell you what she told me about the day she would leave me.

One day I will leave you.

I protested.

"No, no— don't leave me; don't leave us."

She looked at me with big sad eyes and told me a story about a place like no other place we had been to before in this valley— a twice upon a life time place where what looks like safety may be dangerous and what looks dangerous may be just an amazing opportunity for a horse to learn about itself.

When I asked her how she knew, she just shook her mane and continued on with her story.

You know, we are warned to stay away from wild horses born to kicking, nipping, whinnying-at families because those young horses repeat the unsuccessful behaviors of their parents. And they are not good companions to be with.

Well, there was one born to such a family and I stayed out of his way because he was one of the wildest most discontented colts I had ever known but one day he changed.

He looked at me with his big black sad eyes and somehow I guessed he knew something the rest of us didn't know.

His demeanor, his behavior had changed. He was patient and peaceful even with his rude and rambunctious family members. He didn't react violently, didn't retaliate with bites or kicks even when he was attacked.

I was astonished and asked him what happened. He was reluctant to tell me. He said he tried to tell others. They just laughed at him; told him to go swish his tale someplace else.

He looked so sad. I fell in love with him but that's another story.

He told me about a place of verberating crystals and a strange glow that lit up a chamber deep inside a mountain he named Possibility. He said it is a place to discover what you know about yourself.

His family and the horses they run with, drowned out his stories with wild whinnies and wouldn't even consider that there might have been some truth there in Possibility Mountain for them too.

I was the only one who heard what he was saying, who didn't laugh at his story.

Colt's mother was not blinking an eye. She was swishing her tail but otherwise standing very still, in a wide-awake trance—transmitting to Colt:

"What is it like? That place?" I asked your grandmother.

She said, "I had almost forgotten about our magical places. But that wild horse's tale reminded me that I knew about it—where it was and how to get there. (We forget many things when we are born into this valley world.)"

Colt's mother flicked her tail again.

Your grandmother said, "One step into it— the tones, the music can be so beautiful. A whole complete cord was vibrating my body. And the light, the light—"

I asked her, "What light?"

She just said, "One day, you may need to go there. You will recognize it. A place where there is no sun or moon and yet the light is so bright, at first it is blinding. Sounds there can be disorienting."

Colt's mother stopped transmitting. She paused for a moment before she went on with the story. She looked around at where she was standing. Her nostrils flared and she took a deep breath.

"Now, I see and hear what grandmother knew. It is so!"

Colt reared up and transmitted to his mother.

"I found it on my own hoofs. I'm not afraid."

Colt's mother threw her head and shook her mane. Your grandmother warned me.

"You may think you are brave but *you will have to face your fears—down certain hallways.*"

I can hardly believe it but she said, "A white panther may cross your path one day. Watch out for it."

I saw a white panther cross your path today, Colt. Yet, I am not discouraging you. Grandmother didn't discourage me.

She urged me to go on and to remember about horses deciding to be born, coming into this world to explore life and themselves. One day (if it is meant to be) they stumble into a place that goes deeper and deeper inside the mountain.

If they find themselves going down a hallway blocked by invisible barriers, that's when they will learn something new about themselves and they will find another way home.

I loved your grandmother's stories but I whinnied to her.

"I'm afraid; without you I don't know how I'll face my fears."

"You will do it," your grandmother whinnied back to me. "Horses already know what they need to know. It's built-in, hard-wired core knowledge and not just in horses—in all beings."

I know you don't really need a mother horse to tell you to go on, Colt but:

If you find yourself holding your breath, going into frightening, strange places, hesitate for a few moments. Be still and just breathe. Count your breaths until you are calm and then you will know how to go on—how to take the next step.

On the other side of sad and discouraged is a door and through it—more than what you are looking for. Something bigger and better than you could have imagined for yourself is there. The surprising, miraculous story only you can tell, is waiting for you. You are meant to tell it to our family of ears.

One day, tears came to your grandmother's eyes and she said, "It is not easy for me to say goodbye to you, Fair Maiden Horse, even though I know once upon a time and a long time ago before you were born, we agreed—you and I— that it would be so."

"Don't go," I begged her.

She whinnied.

"When you do not see my horse form, I am still with you. We will meet again. Through one of your senses, you will hear— see— feel— taste— or smell me,"

I didn't understand—stamped my hoofs, swished my tail and threw my head. It didn't help. I still remember her last words.

"Remember stories! Your stories! Our horsestories!"

The next day, your grandmother walked with her head held high and her tail swishing, right into the valley pasture beneath the Sharpie's cave. I watched day after day as she grazed in the valley ever closer to the Sharpie's cave until I decided, I had better things to do and I went off with the other colts and found your father.

She did disappear one day and never returned to the herd. At odd times I remember her stories—at the taste of sweet grass, at the sound of bubbling in the fountain, at the smell in the air after a rain.

Colt's mother blinked an eye. She was coming out of her trance. Her thinking shifted to the present when she heard "Caw, Caw."

The black bird—what about it is so familiar?

She took a deep breath and was back in a trance—not transmitting this time just contemplating.

Did the Sharpie and my mother agree a long time ago—the when-time she would—

Colt was remembering some of the herd who didn't have stories told to them—how they taunted him.

They're just made up horsestories—couldn't be true.

Colt threw his head to one side *and* looked his mother in the eye, as he transmitted.

Now I know from my own experience, the truth of our horsestories. Grandmother's stories are true. We can stand in the pink chamber of light. We can hear the music with our own ears.

Colt's mother nudged him.

"I love you, Colt. I'm glad I found you again down this hallway, before you faced the dangers of this place. Your grandmother not only knew about this place, she must have been here."

Colt transmitted.

"When we get back to Storytelling Place, even the most skeptical horses in the herd surely must believe us. We are witnesses. There is more than a one horse proof, this time."

Precious, Dreamer, Talking Horse, the Wizard and the crow were breathing with Colt's mother, and Colt. They were knowing what was being transmitted between the two.

In the silent pregnant pause, first one opened a mouth and then another and another and in one strange mixed up voice it was said to many ears:

Something brings us together in this inner glowing place of learning.

They could almost hear a whisper of verberations from the pink chamber that sounded like *discovering— loving— one another in the oneness.*

A voice inside them echoed the thought of oneness in a word that sounded like—*Namaste*

Four-headed Beast

"An invisible barrier turned us around," said Dreamer.

"It sounds like a mixture of fear and love brought the colt's mother," said The Wizard.

"All that inner talking, I didn't think she would ever stop," said Talking Horse.

"We came to help you and to help Colt's mother," said Precious.

The Wizard looked at Precious and then closed his eyes. A picture came to him. He saw her looking out a window of her castle tower bedroom.

He was smiling to himself. He lifted his elbows away from his body—almost as if he had wings to flap. His thoughts were soaring. He mumbled.

"It's coming back to me."

The black bird on his shoulder hopped sideways, lifted its wings. The Wizard looked around at it. He shook his head.

"Now what am I going to do with you?"

The bird flew from his shoulder and on down the passageway.

"Caw Caw Caw," was all it could say.

Precious and Dreamer dismounted and found themselves again in one another's arms and in the tender longing that welled up inside them. Their eyes met and then their lips. Precious melted against him. Dreamer held Precious close. She pressed closer.

He said, "I didn't know I could miss you so much."

Colt nosed his mother.

Talking Horse said, "Let's look again at that invisible barrier."

The Wizard lagged behind as the horses followed the crow to the place that kept them from going on.

Colt turned his head—almost pressed one eye up to the barrier. *"What is all that stuff in there?"*

Still hand in hand, Precious and Dreamer stretched to look around Colt and over his head to see through the barrier—to see what Colt was looking at.

"The ceiling and the walls look like they are crying tears," said Precious.

And just then she glanced at Colt, again. She noticed the spot around his eye. In Panther Corridor light it looked red to her.

"YNNALINE! YNNALINE! The healing liquid!" she shouted. "We'll find it behind that barrier. By my grandmother's lullaby, I know it."

The Wizard stood beside Precious and Dreamer at the invisible barrier. It rumbled and grumbled and slowly lifted.

"What are we looking at?" Dreamer asked the Wizard.

"This chamber holds advanced technology," he said.

"Is the beast dangerous?"

The Wizard shook his head.

"No, not if you understand it is just a robot, a metal Simpleton following instructions—programmed somewhere, some other when. The liquid it manufactures seems to be ever so versatile, almost magical. If I only knew more about it."

"Did you bring Ynnaline to my Castletown, once upon a long time ago?" Precious interrupted the Wizard.

"No, I don't think so. I didn't know Castletown had any of this magical potion until you mentioned it, just now."

"I am still experimenting with it here and in another time you couldn't relate to without some kind of bridge to it. You wouldn't understand our technology."

" I did go down another hallway once and ended up in a time-space a bit like but not quite the same as your Castletown."

"It is curious. Now, I wonder how many others have come close to this bottled magic—have been afraid to reach out for it. How many others even held it in their hands and did not know what to do with it."

" How many have uncorked what's inside—have tasted a few drops of exhilaration? It was nearly empty—the bottle I found. The few drops on my tongue transported me, peaked my curiosity, allowed me to find—"

Precious interrupted the Wizard again.

"My grandmother said a caravan stopped at their tented encampment at the oasis that was to become Castletown. A strange merchant, traveling with the caravan gave her a bottle filled with a precious liquid."

"She said it was not unusual for desert travelers to carry such gifts with them to repay the hospitality of those who might offer them rest and refreshment. She didn't guess that liquid, would become a healing potion, would save Castletown from a plague. And she didn't guess it would disappear one day."

The Wizard was shaking his head, yes, speaking hesitantly.

"A present from a visitor a long time ago—yes, but here time is always present and past, and future. It just is."

"You go down a hallway and suddenly what you do in the future—can change the past."

Precious shook her head, *no,* so vigorously her hair was swirling. There was an incredulous tone to her voice.

"What are you saying?"

"Here, I remember being Onemug and yet Onemug's time might be described as the distant future of your Castletown."

"In my future, your time is remembered time and in this place perhaps, the very nature of time changes our lives. An ancient scroll from some time frame unknown to me has already changed my past and my future."

"How could that be?" asked Talking Horse.

The Wizard pointed.

"Do you see this crow? She was once the monstrous, the dangerous Sharpie and in my future time she is much more than that."

He waved his hands in the air. The crow flew around his head—watching his hand movements. She was dizzy trying to watch every move he made. The Wizard whispered to her.

"You are a little dizzy now and you would like to sit down."

He pointed to his shoulder. The crow ruffled her wings and cawed and stamped her feet and reluctantly sat down on the Wizard's shoulder.

"She is not used to her new status yet, and I don't know if she remembers that other space-time a long time ago in the future—the beautiful young lady, the brilliant schemer she was."

"That is until she drank more than a few drops of that magic liquid. She ignored my pleas, laughed at my warnings and disappeared from that time."

The crow squawked a short protesting *Caw*.

The Wizard stroked her black feathers.

"Beautiful Sharie, monstrous Sharpie, crow, be still until I stumble across the answers, until I find the magic that goes beyond shrinking your fears to restore you to the perfect being you are. You are not meant to be a crow."

The Wizard's brow was wrinkled as he spoke to Dreamer and Precious.

"One day she will be all that she can be. Perhaps her transformation begins in this valley of horses. For now, she stays with me. If she comes to her senses now she will only know herself as a cranky, foot stomping, cawing crow."

The crow let out two protesting *caw, caws* and then she decided to close her eyes and ears to what was going on around her.

Talking Horse backed away from what looked to him like the flailing of a Four-Headed Beast.

"It may be a simpleton but it still looks dangerous to me."

The Wizard patted Talking Horse.

"It isn't advanced enough to know we are here. Its intelligence is probably more like some of our unconscious intelligence—already pre-scripted for automatic responses."

The Wizard seemed to be slipping into a meditation. His eyes were unfocused, his voice fading away. There were long pauses between his words.

"Beginning to guess— computer like— Mechanism inside— Transcriptions— Erasures— Over-writing?— Creating reconciling?— New?— Old?— Language— Metaphors— Keys— broad— encompassing the dimensions of understanding—a whole— or Holy hologram?"

Precious jumped into his meditation, calling out to him.

"Now that we have stepped inside, beyond the entrance barrier, might we be trapped here, in this chamber?"

The Wizard came back to his senses quickly.

"No, once you are inside, there is no barrier. Don't think of it as a one-way barrier. You can go back through it—at any time you choose."

Precious tossed her head back, brushed hair away from her eyes.

"HOW did you lift the barrier long enough for us to enter?"

The Wizard stroked his beard.

"No, no— I didn't lift the barrier. I don't know how to do that. Only the Simpleton, the robot has the key to who may enter. "

"Somehow it knows who to let in. Unprepared, visitors may stumble down this hallway, but may not enter the chamber. If it is not the proper time, if they have not caught up to the entry event in their lifetime, then the Simpleton darkens the barrier."

"It might look like there is no way to go on. The hallway might appear to be a dead end. If they only knew about timing, about waiting a few more hours, a few more days—the adventure waiting for them."

He paused for a few moments, remembering.

"It is better to come into the Simpleton's chamber before sipping the Simpleton's liquid. I did it backwards—enduring the acceleration the fright, the confusion and sometimes the feeling of despair on my trip to this dimension."

"I think all that is not necessary and I have come up with a theory about how to travel here. I suspect many others might have already reached, might have already returned to this place again and again."

The Wizard looked around at his attentive audience and took a deep breath. He sounded a little like a professor when he resumed speaking.

"A kind of quest begins the journey. It's easier to arrive, to cross the barrier (but not absolutely necessary) if you know the chamber is here."

"Then a kind of inner harmony determines the specifics of a materialization. In other words, you must ask for help and the kind of help you ask for determines the journey you might take."

"Once you are *here*, there is one other requirement for participating in the magic—a willingness to be the vehicle for a transmission."

"What's bottled up wants to be used, to be uncorked. A healing potion wants to be tasted and carried back and forth thru time by those who can carry it off."

Precious was drinking in every word that the Wizard spoke when a question bothered her.

"Could it be Ynnaline? Could our healing potion be the same as your magical sipping liquid ?"

"I'm guessing it might be."

"So many bottles to take home," said Dreamer.

Transporters

The travelers left the Simpleton's chamber and continued down the hallway to a heart shaped chamber.

"Curved ceiling, metal hats, all in a row, on a shelf— who wears those hats?" Precious asked the Wizard.

"I do and you can," said the Wizard. "Put one on. It carries a many storied light but you won't even know it is there until you need it."

"What are you saying?" asked Precious.

"The light will shine. Wait for it. After you get through a dark place, your light will shine brighter and you will be able to see farther than you ever imagined you could. Just be still and wait for the light."

"How am I going to go anywhere, from here?" said Dreamer. "

"A transporter— clear dome transporters are nearby, waiting. They look a little like huge clam shells. Some are large, some are small. I rode in one to a golden clearing and a golden lake, one day."

Dreamer and Precious looked at one another.

"So that's what it was."

The Wizard patted his hat.

"It's a good thing to wear even if you are not riding a transporter. Transporters don't always drop you off at the central chamber— sometimes far out and a long way back."

"One day, I saw another transporter dropping off a king while my transporter slowed down but went right by it. The other transporter must not have been tall enough for the king to wear his crown in it because he was carrying his crown in one hand and a blue book in his other hand."

"I saw him standing there looking forlorn and alone. It looked like nowhere to me. Suddenly steps appeared— twelve moving steps. He stepped up onto the first step. It looked like the steps were carrying him to a light filled gathering place, a welcoming place where everyone had a blue book. Someone was calling to the king— *Just for today.*

"As my transporter was carrying me away, I thought I heard someone say— *anonymous*. At that dropping off place *anonymous* must have initiated a kind of magical *disappearing spell* because when I looked back, I saw nothing, not even a trace of where the king stood."

The light in the Wizard's hat flickered. Precious pointed at it.

"It's a signal. A transporter is on its way," said the Wizard.

The adventurers were exploring deeper and deeper into a heart shaped super-learning chamber. The Wizard pointed.

"See these chairs. I have names for some of them:

The Chair of Remembrance –

The Chair of Clearing the Way –

The Chair of Opening a Book of Life and Reading It."

Precious and Dreamer sat in a chair. The Wizard spoke.

"You are safe wearing your hat. Feel the chair touching your body. (His words were slowing down.) Hear the sounds around you—the sounds of your own breathing. Now breathing in— breathing out— feel the pulses of life in your body. Allow the magic of breathing together."

Precious looked at Dreamer. He looked at her. They were sitting in The Chair of Remembrance.

The Wizard spoke more slowly—reassuringly.

"You can really *open your eyes.* Imagine taking two steps away from yourself—going back, back to a time before you were born."

The Wizard waited for Precious and Dreamer to take a few deep breaths.

"It can be comfortable to—*see* guides and old friends again—planning *the events* of your life unfolding Now—frame the picture. *Take a deep breath. A line drawn across a round table is your life line.*"

The Wizard's voice had been rising and falling like waves in the ocean. Finally he spoke in a conversational tone.

"When you are ready, sit down around the round table with guides and friends and see the steps you may take. You are choosing your parents and who will test your patience. You have decided to take these steps together."

"It is a synergistic lifetime advancing the wisdom of all participants included in it. You may have been a parent to those who will parent you this time."

The Wizard's voice took on a determined almost commanding tone.

"*This Time You Can Remember*—entering into a lifetime together, choosing to experience lessons. Know yourself— learning how to *love.*"

Only Dreamer and Precious were in the Chair of Remembrance but the other adventurers were almost in a trance, listening to the Wizard's words.

"Look down the line until you come to *now*. See, you are carrying your own light. You illuminate the pictures in *your life story* and the pictures have their own inner light. When you are peaceful and centered, the light is soft and not glaring."

"You can give others *the gift* you are meant to bring them. In this chair, a few minutes is equal to a lifetime."

"It is refreshing to learn at your own pace—the right way. Now you *know* what you know and you *come back here, now.* You are *able to describe* what you have learned."

There was just the sound of breathing together.

Talking Horse said, "Are you asleep or awake?"

The Wizard said, "Everyone of us is wider awake now."

Clearing The Way Chair

Dreamer looked down at his feet and squeezed the arm of the chair.

"I know I am sitting in a chair. My feet are on the ground."

Precious was pointing at another chair—The Chair of Clearing the Way.

"What happens in that chair?"

The Wizard shook his head as if he were trying to clear his own thoughts.

"It was like riding on a beam of light again—the first time I sat in that chair. It was like I was back there in an uncomfortable, embarrassing experience."

"Pictures rolling again—we were just sitting down to the dinner table—my mother and father, wife and our children. I heard my wife's scolding voice again."

He let the baby-sitter stay out past midnight. He gave her the key. He shouldn't have done that. She was with a stranger, a boy she met at the beach. He should have known better.

"I winced."

The Wizards eyes were like slits and he was a little hunched over as if there were punches to his belly.

"The sound, the tone of criticism in her voice and those shaming words in front of my parents and my children cut me like a knife."

"Pain, I felt a sharp pain in my gut and lower back, and in my right shoulder, my neck. I held my breath."

A tear rolled down his left cheek.

"I looked around the table. Everyone was looking down at dinner plates as empty, as the embarrassed silence. I didn't want to look into my mother's eyes."

" I glanced at my father. There was a kind of helpless dismay in his eyes. Suddenly something about the pictures shifted. I was seeing them but I was re-experiencing the scene as if I were inside my mother."

"My wife's words were a tightness in my mother's chest and then a stabbing pain in her left shoulder."

"Mother was holding her breath. She was watching my father brace himself. He tensed his muscles as if waiting for the next blow."

"When I was inside myself again, I just wanted to close my eyes and go to sleep. It was almost too much for me to process."

As the Wizard was telling his story, he seemed to age. Lines in his face drooped. He groaned and seemed to grow weary. His voice was slow and deliberate as he went on.

And then— and then this time I not only felt, I saw Tok-A-Nok-A biting my ear and holding one hairy paw over my mouth. It was pushing me down with the other paw. I thought I must be asleep and dreaming.

The Chair shook me violently and it shouted, "*WAKE UP!*"

As the Wizard said *wake up* his liveliness returned and he touched his ear, pulled his ear lobe.

Tok-A-Nok-A was not only biting my ear, she was kicking and punching under the table. I could see her there. An angry hungry monster with saw-teeth in an open mouth, was ready to bite.

I screamed, "*HELP!* " And I thought I heard the dining room table say, "*Saints preserve my wood. We need Be-Won-At-Won. Call her.*"

The Wizard paused in the midst of his story, as if he were still amazed at hearing that voice. Then he spoke again.

I was observing it all as if I were outside myself and so I just asked the dining room table(as if it were an ordinary thing to do), "Who is this *Be-Won-At-Won?*"

" *Don't you know? The invisible Resorceress, helps all who call out to her,*" the table replied.

Then the Chair I was sitting in spoke.

"*Take a deep breath and ignore her monstrous teeth, her critical tone of voice. Tok-A-Nok-A will shrink unless it drinks more contentious thoughts (thy oughts and ought-nots) unless it is fed more critical and defiant words.*"

The Wizard was silent for a few minutes—taking deep breaths. And then he was inspired.

I was taking deep breaths. I touched the growing peaceful place inside me and learned about myself.

Precious, Dreamer, Talking Horse were all taking deep breaths—breathing with the Wizard.

The Wizard spoke again.

Be-Won-At-Won appeared and then she jumped into moving pictures of the replayed event. She pulled me into the pictures too and allowed me to manipulate them. I watched her slow the pictures down.

When we were both in a still frame, she rolled her eyes and tilted her head until I noticed a paw-hand around my wife's eyes and another around her throat.

It was Tok-A-Nok-A but this time Tok-A-Nok-A was losing its grip in the presence of Be-Won-At-Won. With her help, I was able to step into the other moving pictures and slow them down and change them—one frame at a time. I slowed one frame enough so that my mother had time to speak.

Mother asked my wife, "*Was the girl hurt? Did she betray your confidence in her?*"

My wife just shook her head, *no.* I got up from the table stood beside my wife and put my arm around her. My mother had a look of relief on her face.

I said to my wife, "*I regret—I'm sorry I didn't know that something still frightens you even though everything turned out all right.*"

The monster heard, *I regret and I'm sorry* and lost its grip. My wife slipped out of the monster's hold in those few moments.

I looked directly at the monster and said, *"You can stop that right now because everything turned out all right."*

My father looked me in the eye and smiled.

In a gentle tone of voice I said to my wife, what I was unable to say before, *Nothing unexpected, nothing bad happened. You and I have confidence in the baby-sitter. She didn't disappoint us.*

She has common sense and maturity beyond her years. We have both noticed her good judgment and self restraint. Isn't that why we trust her to be with our children?

I realized, then, if I had been more observant I might have caught a glimpse of Tok-A-Nok-A sooner. I might have welcomed her and thanked her. Even though she was mistaken in her method, she was trying to get us to a better place— to a place of understanding and peaceful oneness.

The Wizards face relaxed—the frown, the wrinkles in his forehead were almost gone. The Wizard was smiling—a twinkle in his eye as he spoke about Tok-A-Nok-A again.

.

Tok-A-Nok-A was still trying to hide from us under the table when Be-Won-At-Won whispered to me, *"Tell your wife the monster under the table is just fear from another time and it is a monster because it is out of place, here."*

A whirrrring simpleton, the four-headed mechanical beast drowned out the sound of the travelers breathing together in the magical heart shaped chamber. The Wizard raised his voice and spoke over the din.

My wife's mouth dropped open as Be-Won-At-Won became visible. She paused in the middle of her words. A tear rolled down her cheek.

She sighed in wordless wonder as Be-Won-At-Won put her arms around us. We were hugged and then set free.

Be-Won-A-Won waved her wand. Tok-A-Nok-A was transformed and put in her proper place, in another time—in an empty frame waiting for her.

She was enclosed in it and became visible—the fearful desperate very young girl, very pregnant, too soon, before she was ready to take care of a baby.

There were tears in Dreamer's eyes and in Precious' eyes as they pictured the awful plight of a child about to become a mother. Talking Horse was lifting one foot and putting it down again.

There was a catch in the Wizard's voice.

"Be-Won-At-Won waved her wand.

No more monsters! No more under the table fears! No more sawing on innocent tables and chairs! All that's left of that monster is the tale it drags behind it.

I almost laughed when I found myself again—in this safe hat, in this magical chair. My eyes opened wider.

"Now you can experience inner peacefulness," said Talking Horse. "I experience inner peacefulness too but it didn't come from sitting in that chair. When I was afraid, Dreamer helped me know what I didn't know I knew."

"*Perhaps Dreamer helps me too,*" murmured the Wizard to himself.

"It seems we all have our own purposes here," said Precious.

Dreamer touched his hat.

"I feel like a miner with this hat on. Perhaps we'll dig up a treasure or two down some dark passageway."

Treasure

"Yes, wear this hat. With its light, a measure of safety goes with you," said the Wizard. "Be sure to notice even a slight flickering. Flickering light made itself known to me—one time at the edge of a mysterious darkness (Before I stepped all the way into it.) I stopped just in time."

"Flickering? Couldn't you see? Is that what stopped you?" Precious asked.

"I was overcome with panic, in the momentary darkness. I held my breath and I must have closed my eyes but, thank goodness, I waited."

"In a few moments, when I opened my eyes again, I caught sight of another flashing beam of light over my head and I had an overwhelming urge, to reach out to it. I knew it wasn't a logical thing to do but I did it. I lifted my eyes and my arms above my head and stretched and took a deep breath."

"I stood with my arms above my head and the feeling of panic that was welling up inside me subsided and my eyes accommodated. An occasional glimpse of light overhead, enabled me to see how to go on."

"Now when I am discouraged or feeling down, I stretch and take a deep breath and reach over my head. My helmet light responds, becomes brighter. I found out it is impossible to be depressed or in a panic for long with your hands raised above your head. Who could have guessed that something so simple—? *Remember that position.*

Onemug sounded like a professor lecturing.

It wasn't long after I had already experienced the effect of that body pose, that I read about it. Someone at the university (in the psychology department) wrote a paper about it in a time you might consider your future. And isn't that wonderful? It looks like light answers requests in every time, in any time, in no particular time at all.

The Wizard was standing there, arms spread, elbows at his sides palms up, as if her were waiting for all to realize the significance of another great discovery. Finally he spoke again.

I think the universe wants us to know—it is ready and willing to give us a kind of coincidental reassurance that we know what we know. But, I am diverging from my story; aren't I?

When I had enough light to go on, somehow I knew I should count my breaths. I counted my breaths, until I felt I was breathing in from my toes and then all the way up into my head and even out beyond my head and then back in again and down to my toes.

Then my light really revived—was growing so strong it was shining again on the ceiling of the passageway. The ceiling reflected my light and shined back its own reassuring soft beam of light.

The thought that I might have taken that big misstep into a dark pit, that some other missteps might lay ahead for me was daunting but I knew the right thing for me to do was to go on.

I would wait for whatever light might be up ahead to make itself known to me. I took deep breaths and watched my steps.

Going on—the few simple steps I took led me to other hallways. As my eyes adjusted, I was seeing deeper into one passageway after another and down one passageway I could see a Castletown and white and black horses.

When I stepped foot into the passageway, it was dark—night time there. It seemed to me I flew somewhere and worked all night.

At dawn, I knew I had completed some task but I knew it was not my way or my time and a little out of place for me then.

It seemed to me that I escaped through some window and then I landed (That's the only way I can describe it.) in that passageway again and headed back down the hallway to where I came from.

Watching my steps, on the way back I avoided falling into another pit. It was a big one. There was a wooden ladder stashed nearby and an interesting huge old battered chest down there but the more I thought about the retrieval struggle—the strength it might take to open it up and then carry what I found back with me, the more I realized I didn't want to do it at that time.

It might have been too exhausting and time consuming for me. Something urged me on. I had a feeling there were more important things to do and I was on my way to them.

Precious was suddenly excited and interrupted the Wizard.

"Which passageway was it? Do you remember the way that led to Castletown and black and white horses?"

Dreamer had a quizzical look on his face and he asked Precious, "Do you want to go back there?"

Dreamer turned his attention to the Wizard and asked, "How do we know our lights will last—won't flicker when we come to the pits? How do we know we won't fall into one? What if we decide to go down into a pit? Maybe that treasure you didn't take waits for us to find it."

The Wizard had a thoughtful look on his face. His left hand was around his chin.

"It may be there for someone like you. I don't know. I don't remember how to get back to the pit or to the hallway that led to that Castletown. I just know that I was there at the threshold to both places."

The Wizard paused and then continued on as if he had not been interrupted.

I don't know what anyone else might find there or what might be carried back and how hard it might be to climb out of a pit, once you are there. I was glad when a transporter showed up.

I was ready for a rest and I thought it might be a quicker way to get to where I wanted to go but when it stopped at each station, I looked around and I wasn't where I wanted to be—nothing familiar.

It wasn't returning me to the pit or to Castletown or the Central Chamber, just some unfamiliar places I didn't want to, didn't have time to investigate if I wanted to get on with—what I guessed, what I was beginning to believe was an important mission for me.

Perhaps some transporters have regular routes and some just stop at random places. I don't know. I finally had to disembark again to find my own way back here. I'm so glad I was wearing this hat.

The Wizard raised both hands above his head and stretched and then put his hand to his head to make sure the hat was still there.

Transporters took me to dark places and to places of light. I haven't found any maps to its routes. I'm still observing and learning the ways of this place.

Choices

"Some Wizard you are," said Precious.

"A wizard is only a wizard to those who don't know what a wizard knows. Anyone can know, can learn to be still, to find the passageways and perhaps even the treasures and magic in this place, in any place. A little coincidence, a little curiosity, the right effort at the right time and you are the Wizard," he said.

"I walk beside what is precious to me," said Dreamer.

"You hold hands with the key to unlocking your destiny," the Wizard said to Precious.

"Who knows where we will go and what we will do together?" said Dreamer.

"It is perhaps more than even a Wizard can know," said Precious.

Precious and Dreamer put their foreheads together and whispered for a while. Precious looked longingly into ancient eyes.

"I would like to restore the magic Ynnaline to Castletown so that what was lost is found as it was written in our nursery rhymes and sung in our lullabies. I would like to find another place, another *sumwhere* we could be together, forever after, Dreamer."

"I was hoping you would want to stay with me. Together, we can find a way."

Precious reached her arms around Dreamer and snuggled against his body and kissed him on the cheek.

He pulled her close to him—closer and closer. His longing grew into a kind of knowing about incompleteness, an incompleteness that was made whole with Precious beside him. For the first time, Dreamer knew anguish and the longing and tenderness of his protective love for Precious. He stroked her hair and then held her face in his hands and stared and stared at her as if he were trying to memorize every one of her features.

"Have we come into a chamber of no-time, where travelers may tarry a while to exchange the knowledge of different times?" Dreamer asked Precious.

"When we leave this chamber, will time ever bend again and allow us to come together in this place?" Precious asked Dreamer.

Dreamer and Precious decided to confide in the Wizard. They would ask him what they should do.

"I don't know what you should do. I don't give advice about shoulds," said the Wizard. "You could sit in the Chair of Opening The Book Of Life And Reading It and see where it takes you. You could formulate a plan—find tools and learn how to use them to transport the magic Ynnaline back to your Castletown."

"We already know that the unique containers in this dimension— in this here and now— pass thru time unharmed. Perhaps they can, perhaps you can travel down more than one time hallway and become—"

Precious interrupted the Wizard again.

"Could it be that no one steals the liquid Ynnaline, that it is where it is supposed to be at any one time, that it always comes from the heart of a beast—that this beast encourages us, some of us to take a bottle or two because it is needed somewhere, some when? Perhaps it puts the magic elixir, the bottled liquid in our hand when—"

She interrupted herself.

"We must find the way back to Castletown!"

"Yes, that sounds right," said Dreamer.

He was staring at the mysterious Chair Of Opening The book Of Life And Reading It.

It had a strange kind of writing on it.

The Wizard said, "Aha you have noticed what is written there. I copied it down and took it back with me to my future and had some scholars of ancient texts, translate it for me. They said it translates to—no past, no present, no future."

Dreamer questioned the Wizard.

"Where will it take us?"

The Wizard shifted his gaze up and to the right. He stood there staring into space before he replied.

There is no map—nowhere but perhaps a how to get to where you want to go. When you sit in the chair you will be here and there.

There you are outfitted in proper clothing for the journey and you may not realize it but there is a transparent protective magnetic field, an invisible body shield that even penetrates your clothing, that shines out a kind of light that allows you to see thru new eyes, hear thru new ears and to feel in a new dimension.

You will find yourself in a strange new-old place. Do not be afraid. As a wise man once said, "*There is nothing to fear but fear itself.*"

The place you travel to is a place where truths otherwise impossible to know, become known to you.

Remember! When you get back to Castletown choose your words carefully. You may frighten others, if you tell them what you have seen and heard here because they are not yet ready to understand.

One day they will and I believe we can and everyone will at the proper time— discover this place for themselves.

We'll all cross barriers we thought we could not cross to find a way home to a real time, a real *sum-where* place for all of us.

What we do here might sound like fairy tales to the uninitiated. For now, for your own protection keep this real-virtuality seating place a secret and be like the Simpleton. Wait for the right time, the right place to communicate—to give your gift, perhaps to be the gift.

You are a part of the universal consciousness now and you are almost ready to take your own unique journey to where no one has gone before. Be alert. Study what interests you. Go to the library.

There is a librarian to help you find what you are looking for. Ask for help and you will get it.

"What if we lose our way? Will we know when or how to find our way back here?" asked Dreamer.

"I don't know . I only know I have found my way back many times and once just in the nick of time. It can test your own ingenuity," said the Wizard.

The Real-Virtuality Chair, Dreamer and Precious sat in was big enough for two.

"We journey together," they said.

Dreamer and Precious were holding hands, leaning shoulder to shoulder and then they were somewhere else.

"What are you doing?" asked Talking Horse.

Precious and Dreamer did not respond to his question.

The Quest

"They have begun a quest," said the Wizard. "They journey in another dimension. It looks like you might still talk to them and touch them but an invisible partition separates the dimensions."

Talking Horse walked up to Dreamer and Precious. Before he reached them his nose bumped into an invisible barrier.

"How do you know about this place, the devices here and that chair?" the horse asked the Wizard.

"I have been coming back to this place again and again—listening, feeling the rhythms of the automaton, watching it work. I have been watching, waiting, learning, waiting some more, expecting and I think expecting has something to do with it—the coincidences that lead to our discoveries."

One day I grew weary (and I think it was more than by chance) I sat down on that inviting comfortable seat to rest a few minutes. I was still wondering what I was waiting for when I heard voices coming from deep inside myself.

What are you doing here? You may travel and teach. You may visit the library and learn. You may experiment with devices to benefit fellow travelers. Choose!

I was surprised, pleasantly and not at all questioning the experience. I pondered the choices presented to me. I thought I might like to visit another time—bring advantages and advances to a developing culture. As I was thinking—*but I would need a guide*—wonder of all wonders a page, a young man from a Castletown walked up to me and took my hand and led me.

At first I didn't realize, I was in two places at once—here and in another dimension. The other dimension was so real to me this place seemed like a dream and I didn't even question how I knew about more advanced technologies.

The page called me, Merlin and said he was pleased to announce my presence to the king and queen and all the court of Camelot.

I was dressed in wise man garb, pointed hat and long flowing robe. It was as if they were expecting me. I advised the king and taught the royal children.

Eventually the memory of this launching place and the chair in this room came back to me and then the memory of where I come from—the work I did at the university returned as well. Unfortunately or perhaps fortunately, technology and the comforts I was accustomed to did not transfer to Camelot with me.

I had great difficulty manufacturing even one match, a simple fire making device, a common essential taken for granted in my lifetime at the university. It was fun being a magician but I was asked to do more and more, too much.

I was beginning to suspect my presence could actually retard some developments in that culture's learning curve and necessary personal skills. Instead of finding their own answers, I was expected to know the answer to every question. It was a wearying responsibility and I began to make plans to leave.

I wrote about my experiences in Camelot—left scrolls about my life here, about the Sharpie, about my Onemug existence and about you, Talking Horse. I left them underneath the king's throne—hidden, carefully rolled and fitted into a carved cedar box.

As I was placing them there, a librarian appeared and said, "*Thank you. It is done. Stories sealed with my sealing wax remain invisible until once upon a time's cogent philosophical forays are delivered by lorries to different kinds of quarries. At borders—*"

Suddenly there was a loud wooshing sound and I missed some of her message—could barely hear her voice trailing off.

"*It's a song you can sing, the author's name, the one who will bring—*"

I missed some words but heard clearly.

"*You must go now.*"

Someone took my hand. The librarian nodded yes and turned around and left me. The unexpected guide turned me in a new direction and patted me on the shoulder. As he prodded me to be on my way, he warned me quietly.

"*Another page grows bolder, looking over your shoulder, reading some of what you write on the scrolls. He guesses you are about to leave, and abandon teaching the royal children. A person must know when it is time to go, when the page might alert the king. Royal patrols might be dispatched to be-head you.*"

I had only taken a few steps on my way when I heard the king's horsemen coming after me. I was running down the road again, didn't have time to look back. The path fell away behind me. I kept on going until I was almost breathless. When I finally found my second wind, it felt like my feet were not finding the ground under me. I was so tired, I had to sit down.

Was I surprised! A soft sofa like chair supported my back. A warm breeze gently touched my face. I woke up to a glow in this chamber, to the sounds of Ynnaline being manufactured. I heard the comforting rhythm of the Four-Headed Beast in its programmed movements.

Time Travelers

The Wizard was interrupted by the raspy sound of heavy breathing. Dreamer and Precious stood up and ran over to him—almost out of breath, eyes wide open as if they had had a terrible fright.

"How— what— when— where are we?" said Dreamer and Precious almost in unison.

Precious said, "It felt like a lifetime of traveling—traveling into and back out of Castletown."

"You have been here the whole time," said Talking Horse. "And it was just a few minutes ago that I bumped into an invisible barrier around you, couldn't reach you. You couldn't hear me."

"I was just telling Talking Horse about my adventures in Camelot," said The Wizard. "But, tell us about your journey; it looks like you had a harrowing experience."

"This chamber seemed to disappear as we sat in the Real-Virtuality Seat and then a robed traveler appeared walking beside us," said Dreamer

"We were on a familiar and yet unfamiliar desert trail," said Precious. "And the wanderer asked us: *Where are you going and what do you want to do when you get there*?"

"I want to go home—to return some magic Ynnaline to those who still search for it in Castletown just as it was predicted in our nursery rhymes, in tales my grandmother told me."

"*Things are seldom what they seem*," the companion said. "*What is your intention, here, Dreamer*?"

"I wish to accompany Precious—to protect her on her journey."

"*And! AND*?"

"Yes, you are right. Underneath it all, I hope Precious will want to return with me to another here and now. A *Sum-place* of our adventures together, of discovering our own way through whatever might be on the path ahead of us. I want to be with her, to walk beside her, in front of her, behind her—just so we're together. I'll wait forever for her, if I must."

"*She may not be able to leave Castletown life behind her, if she returns there. Do you realize she may choose to stay with the royal court and its familiar ways*?"

Precious patted Talking Horse on the neck and told him that a tear rolled down Dreamer's cheek and then the traveling companion sighed, paused perhaps giving them some time to think about what was said.

Talking Horse and the Wizard were nodding at what Precious was telling them:

The companion seemed to be looking at a space deep inside our eyes, when finally he said, "*It is a dangerous journey—going back. Not only do re-entries become obscured but some doorways close. Some who journey, forget where they come from*."

He shook his finger at us.

"*Remember the road we are on. Stay awake and remember to remember this way—endings are just a beginning again. Our paths cross many times coming and going. Now close your eyes and begin again*."

When next, I opened my eyes Dreamer was gone. I was a traveler in a caravan. The leader of the caravan was staring at me. Something about the young man attracted me.

The plain cedar box I carried, concealed rare treasures. I knew it was a desert tradition—gift giving to the host and hostess who would provide us with refreshment and repose in the midst of our long journey across the forbidding desert territory.

I was on my way to a sea port, on my way to set sail on a double-mast ship but first, this scorching desert had to be crossed. I knew where I was going but perhaps it was the heat—I kept thinking there was something more I should remember about my destination and this caravan's resting place, something important.

We were headed for an oasis. The caravan would rest there before we continued the journey. My thoughts were spinning: *Why was I reluctant to think about leaving the caravan and the leader of the caravan behind when we reached the sea port?*

I was puzzling about my anxiety and forgetfulness when knights of a royal presence at the oasis came to escort me to the royal tent. I caught a glimpse of myself, a reflection in the polished metal shields the knights carried— *Mustache? Beard?*

I touched my face, stroked my cheek. A sudden gust of wind swirled the sand and as it rose before my eyes, the vision of a castle town seemed to appeared before me. *Was it a mirage rising out of the heat and the sand?*

I glanced at a metal shield again and caught a glimpse of what I was wearing—dusty clothes of a wealthy merchant. Panic—*why was I feeling panic about my appearance?*

As we approached the royal encampment, I expected to see walls and gates and guards on horseback. But, they were not there. I had seen them so clearly, in the mirage, in the rising heat waves. My thoughts were not logical:

What is happening to me?"

The king of this royal encampment was just building a fortress around the deep wells of the oasis. The young king and his bride were dwelling in a beautiful tent of many colors. His knights conducted me into the royal tent. I shook my head as I heard a familiar name—a grandmother's name.

My imagination was running away with me: *Why did I think, a grandmother's name?*

I was introduced to the lovely young queen—much too young to be a grandmother and yet I couldn't help thinking of her as a grandmother.

My head was spinning a little as I opened my plain cedar box and presented the king with its precious content, a bottle of liquid, sealed with a cork with the mark of a sea shell on it.

I heard myself telling him about the bottle and what was in it: *Centuries ago, this medicine was discovered buried in and among the rubble of a collapsed mountainside. We discovered it and have been using it sparingly to heal otherwise incurable diseases. This bottle I present to you is one of the remaining few. Ynnaline is as valuable as pearls in an ocean and as valuable as water in a desert.*

As we discussed the usefulness of the magic Ynnaline, I looked around and noticed a few beautiful black and white horses and the picture of this castle town as it might be constructed flashed in front of my eyes.

I didn't know why these feelings were welling up inside me, overtaking me. My hands were shaking.

I tried to clear my thoughts of the vision but then the king began to explain his plans for the community to be and somehow I already knew what he was going to say—where the castle would stand, where the stable would be.

The pulses of my body were whirling and I had to calm myself, to refrain from exclaiming about what I knew but didn't know how I knew. I struggled to keep silent and calm as the king spoke.

It is strange but I have noticed that as the walls grow higher, as we are building our own protection, the workers grow tired and become ill. Perhaps we have a need for the magic Ynnaline already and good fortune has brought you to our tent.

Even as we were speaking, more and more laborers were falling ill and the laborers were looking for some reason for their illness. I heard what one of them said.

I was well until the strangers arrived in their caravan.

Rumors were soon flying around the encampment. The caravan leader was very observant and he noticed various groups of workers whispering together. As all good leaders do, even though he was not fluent in the desert language, the caravan leader positioned himself so that he might overhear what was being said and so that he might sense what might be in the air.

He sensed danger for his caravan travelers in the staccato tone of voices he heard, followed by head nodding and furtive whispers. He hurried to the royal tent and as I emerged to gaze at the stars that night, he approached me and whispered about what he had observed.

We must leave before the appointed hour and under cover of this night, while the others sleep, if we are to escape from a secret attack. The wall builder's fearful imaginings have turned to wrath against our caravan.

I didn't want to go. What was I thinking? *Something holds me here. The queen, even just her name somehow holds me here—some kind of bond between us.*

The bond was strong. I felt it and I was tired from my travels. I wanted to rest in the beginnings of a new Castletown.

I had this odd feeling: *I belong here. Something is undone and something is finished—no, fulfilled but what is it?"* Ancient eyes—*the leader of the caravan has ancient eyes.* Longing—*no other way to explain the feeling I had looking into his eyes.*

I pondered about my gift giving and their receiving: *Have I told them enough? Will they know how to use it? Yes, yes, somehow I knew they would.*

The caravan leader put his arm around my shoulders. I nearly swooned at his touch. No woman or man had so affected me this way before. I puzzled about it: *What is it about this person that touches me?*

And then there was a momentary hint: *Just a glimpse of the long road ahead of us—a guide leading us somewhere.* I knew we must go. But *we, us*— I didn't know why I was telling myself *us* when he would leave me at the sea port.

While I was contemplating the strangeness I felt in my life, the caravan was resuming its journey—a weary night journey this time away from the colorful tents and on to the sea. As the sun was coming up, shining in our eyes, we looked back. There were clouds of dust, horsemen riding after us again.

Again—I can still see myself riding up beside the caravan leader and asking him, "Has this happened before?"

He said, "*No* and then *yes*." I heard a chime—no a chord, a faint chord of beautiful tones. I was amazed and wondering. I took a deep breath and I sighed as I breathed out, all the way out. And then the landscape changed.

The desert faded away into colored dancing lights, a tunnel of light and I knew he was there with me but not the same person. The leader of the caravan was holding his hand out to me.

No, it was Dreamer beckoning me. I was running to meet him. We were both running down the same road and when we were almost out of breath— here we are!

"I think we were a little off the mark," said Dreamer. "We were a little out of proper time in order to— "

"No, it was exactly right," said Precious. "I know I have done what I could do about what was written in the nursery rhyme. What was lost is found."

"What we do in the future is important. It changes us and how we see the very nature of time and our time together."

"What do you mean?" asked Dreamer.

"We have been set free of time, in time to change ourselves , our histories and herstories and even horsestories. I am eager to explore more hallways with you, Dreamer."

A big smile engulfed Dreamer's face and it was so big The Wizard and Talking Horse caught it and they beamed too.

Then, there was a sound in the chamber. A strange low tone massaged their ear drums and rumbled in the chamber. It shook their bodies and vibrated the mechanical parts of the Four-Headed Beast.

Cracks appeared in the walls. A huge transporter arrived at the back of the chamber. The startled visitors to the chamber hurriedly climbed aboard and they were whisked down a long passageway. The passageway was collapsing behind them. The Wizard stroked his beard, and mused out loud.

"The Four-Headed Beast, Simpleton—does it survive? It is surely crushed or sealed in that chamber. I wonder—"

Re-Questing

Dreamer winked at Precious and said, "Things are seldom what they seem."

Talking Horse swished his tail.

"I wonder where we are going, now?"

"Isn't it awesome that a transporter materialized just when we needed it?" Precious said and she winked at Dreamer.

The other passengers were silent sorting through their own thoughts and watching and waiting—waiting to see what might happen and what might become of them.

Even the crow on the Wizard's shoulder was standing still, not stamping her feet, not crowing. She was craning her neck to see what was whirling by them.

Colt was really enjoying the ride. He noticed his mother was frightened and he nudged her with his nose and tried to reassure her everything would be all right.

After all, we are snug and secure in this transparent clam-shell transporter and we're riding with Talking Horse and the Wizard. What could happen with such wise and experienced travelers alongside us?

He tried to direct his thoughts to his mother but she was too frightened to receive them and in a moment of extreme fright she reared up on her hind legs and bumped her head on the roof of the transporter.

The roof popped open. There was an overwhelming suction—a powerful force pulling the passengers out of the transporter.

Colt and his mother were tumbling in mid-air. The Wizard and the crow disappeared. Talking Horse looked like a prince, like a horse, like a prince.

Dreamer and Precious closed their eyes and held onto one another. They heard.

Second level, storied place, Second Storied Place—

Then they opened their eyes and looked around.

"Did you hear that?" said Dreamer.

"Where are we?" said Precious.

They found themselves in an enclosed but welcoming space. It felt friendly there—mountains in the distance. Fragrant carpet-like grasses were underfoot and there was what looked like a fountain nearby. The pink marble basin for containing water looked like it might have risen from underground, from a squared bed of what looked like pure white gravel.

"I don't know where we are but it seems so familiar somehow," said Dreamer.

"I'm thirsty," said Precious. "There should be water here. I wonder when it will bubble up. Look, there's a hint of a side path. I wonder if there is a golden lake at the trail's end?"

Dreamer took a deep breath and said, "Fruit—apple or maybe it's a peach fragrance in the air and a humming of insects, a buzzing of bees. Look at that!"

Dreamer pointed at four columns made of a crystalline material. He approached one and peered into it. *Looks like something written here— characters embedded in the stone. How could it be? What does it mean?*

He read, "Tell-u-ride—a golden glowing silver chalice overflows. Know that you know. The one who goes deep inside finds the answers. Daylight or sylvan night— it is all right to tell-u-ride, to Tell- u – ride."

The crystal Dreamer always carried in his pocket vibrated.

Did it waken to those words or to my voice?

The crystal column containing the words shook. Dreamer looked at Precious to see if she noticed the vibrations.

"The crystal in my pocket is awake and singing with extra verve. Does it recognize this message in the column? How can a column reciprocate? Does it recognize my crystal? What is awakening?" he spoke out loud.

"It sounds like a riddle to me," said Precious.

"Letters scattered in some crystals—could there be words still deeper in the column and might they make up a whole secret sentence? Is there a key to unlocking this mysterious writing in a column—a forgotten code known in some ancient time?"

Precious was thinking about what Dreamer said. She was about to respond when out of the corner of her eye, she caught sight of some movement. Something was emerging from the ancient woods surrounding this *sum-place* she and Dreamer had been brought to.

Someone, a naked someone, wearing a multi pointed, multi-colored floppy hat was approaching. He was coming closer and closer. That someone was throwing some kind of unfamiliar yet recognizable "rounds" up in the air. He was catching a blur of colors or so it seemed—juggling, catching the round *sum-things* again and again and again.

"He juggles strange balls," said Dreamer.

"No, he juggles more than that," said Precious.

She was seeing thru the blur of colors. Look at the balls and into them. See the moving pictures."

"Living stories," said Dreamer. "I can see the characters move—almost spill out as we watch the balls whiz by."

"Look, look!" said Precious. "Could that be part of your life story I just saw?"

She was pointing as she said, "There goes part of my life story. How could Castletown events be embedded in that spinning ball?"

Just then the juggler let one ball touch another ball. The two balls fell together and then there was only one that seemed to grow.

"Our life story together in the larger ball," Dreamer and Precious said in one surprised voice.

The juggler let another small ball touch the bigger ball and it grew again.

"Something touching our life together," said Precious. The juggler, juggled faster and faster and faster. The inside of the balls became a blur. It was exhausting watching the vortex of swirling images.

Dreamer, the horse seller, sat down beside Precious, the princess. They were momentarily stunned and fascinated—just staring at the balls going around and around and up in the air and back down into the juggler's hand.

"I feel a pulsing in my ears and between my ears from side to side in my head," Precious said.

Dreamer said, "I am dizzy—like I am going around and around a deep well and walking somewhere uphill."

"That wasn't so long ago," said Precious.

"Now I remember—re-member—A juggler!" said Dreamer. "I wouldn't have met you—couldn't have if I hadn't met the juggler, if he hadn't appeared when he did."

Precious reached for Dreamer's hand.

"What do you mean? I thought you said you always dreamed about finding the lost valley, the horses of different colors. You said your grandmother's stories inspired you to find the valley."

I did say that and it is true. But there was also a time I was swirling in anxious and frightening feelings. My father was a good king—did his benevolent thing. I had a happy enough childhood but I didn't want to be like him. I didn't even want to be a prince even though I had already chosen a princess to be my bride

She was a beautiful princess and she knew exactly how to run a kingdom, how to follow all the rules of our castled society. She didn't understand me. She would have no part of leaving home to seek adventure. She found fault with everything I did—everything I said.

She was scolding me in front of my parents instead of working things out with me. I was embarrassed at every opportunity she could grasp to embarrass me.

She was not a wicked person. She was just trying to get me to see things her way in the only way she knew how to do that. Perhaps that's how her parents disciplined her. I don't know. But I could feel her words like rough sandpaper gouging me—wearing me down.

Soon I was questioning myself and my right to be. I thought there might be something dreadfully wrong with me or that I might be going crazy.

I thought I didn't deserve to be a prince. A prince doesn't make others around him so unhappy. I was tired all the time; had to force myself to do common ordinary everyday tasks. I was even thinking about killing myself one day, when the juggler strolled onto our castle grounds.

He was naked except for that silly hat he wears and his antics were so ridiculous, I laughed out loud. As usual, no one was paying any attention to him. It was as if they were blind to his antics.

This day he was not throwing the usual things up in the air and catching them again. He was not doing what everyone expected him to do and so I thought surely someone might notice his nakedness but it was as if he were invisible to the royal court.

He looked at me and winked. He was making outrageous faces—sticking his tongue out and making bird sounds as he danced around picking up imaginary things. Then after he threw something up in the air, he bent his elbows and flapped his arms to show me he wasn't just throwing it up in the air this time. He was giving it wings.

I remember the first time I noticed him running around the castle grounds. We were both young boys then. I asked my mother why he ran around naked. She said that as frail and sensitive as he was, he came from a crude and brutal family. When he wore clothes his bruises and welts and floggings were hidden from us.

She said, "Look at him now. Is there a mark on his body?"

While I was remembering what my mother said, he stepped closer and closer to me. Suddenly he leaned over, (bare butted the court) and whispered in my ear.

"If you are going to kill yourself, make sure you don't kill your body."

He almost danced out of sight—out of the castle grounds as quickly, as unexpectedly as he had come. He left me more than startled. I was dumb-founded. How did he know? What did he mean? Can a person die, without losing his life?

Precious was shaking her head and she said, "You didn't really consider killing yourself; did you?"

Dreamer said, "Yes, yes I did until the naked juggler, juggled something inside me. Something was making another kind of sense to me. I decided to leave my life and what I knew my life was to be. I left my way of thinking about that life behind me."

"You are still a reluctant prince," Precious said to Dreamer.

Dreamer shook his head *yes*.

He almost choked up as he whispered, "*I said goodbye to friends, to relatives, to a way of life. I began another kind of journey through the valley and on to some adventures that challenged me to find my own inner resources. I kept bumping into unexpected help along the way and eventually I found myself and my own way and you, Precious.*"

"It seems you just can't get away from partnering a princess," Precious said with a smile.

Dreamer, the horse seller-prince chuckled to himself and then he said, "You are right, again, of course but I'm having so much more fun this time, Precious Princess, Pearl, Ynnaline."

Just then Precious said, "Oh, oh, admitted Prince, Look! Do you think it's the same juggler who approaches again?"

This juggler threw balls so high in the sky, the balls disappeared. He seemed to have all the time in the world to stretch out his hand—to entice a prince and a princess into a sylvan wood.

Dreamer and Precious were curious about his invitation to follow him. They walked deep into the woods behind the juggler whose feet didn't seem to be touching the ground at all. Finally they came to a clearing.

The juggler appeared to be rising into the air and floating there—wearing a pointed hat with balls of light attached to the points. He pulled the balls from the points and threw them up and away. They stretched out into what looked like rainbows in the sky and then he disappeared.

Standing in a kind of daze, Precious said, "What happened to the juggler?"

Dreamer didn't answer her—just shook his head and showed her his empty open palms.

There was a rustling in the underbrush. A crow was *caw...*
Cawing.

Precious and Dreamer looked around at the clearing where they
stood. It was not one of nature's clearings. It must have been carved
out of the thicket. A round roofed mysterious building stood at the
far end of the clearing and seemed to hold back the thorny bushes. A
heavy carved wooden door was ajar.

"The space inside looks like it might have a sacred feeling to it,"
whispered, Dreamer.

Precious tiptoed through the door and walked around the inside
perimeter of the building—stepping on some special inlaid squares.
She was looking up at light coming through colored glass windows
and she was looking down at light falling on a marble tiled floor.

Dreamer gasped at the glowing light that seem to back-light her
golden blonde hair. Precious had a halo around her head.

She looked down at her feet and said, "I am standing again on the
final resting place, on the last remains of some saints. I sense it."

Suddenly she was dizzy and losing her balance.

The Dreamer, Prince saw her sway and ran to her. He supported
her and then gently lowered her down to the floor of the woodland
temple. Gently, he cradled her in his arms.

He was rocking her as he said, "You were holding your breath;
Breathe! Breathe!"

Precious murmured, "The temple is built over a golden lake. I
don't know how I know it but I do and this place is just in a different
space—somehow part of it and yet not part of it. Everything is
connected."

"The balls, the balls juggled for us are worlds we live on and live
in. We're traveling, traveling on a space ship that carries us around
and across a stream, a milky stream. The path is an arc. We're riding
a knower's arc to where we're at and soon—very soon we come to
a different kind of heavenly reality. Even the stars move to new, to
different places."

Footsteps echoed on the marble floor. A Wizard and a crow were
crossing over the threshold, approaching Precious and Dreamer.

"Listen, listen!" said Precious.

She began to chant and sing the strange words she heard inside herself.

Dreamer's body responded to the sounds.

Om Nama Shivaya— Om Nama Shivaya— Ommm Ommm Ommmmmmmmmm.

Some kind of pulsing, whirling began in different areas of his body. The temple in the forest seemed to hum as it resonated to the sound. Precious, Dreamer, the temple, the forest—all were the chant.

It was like a breathing together, a sighing and singing—breathing as one. A comforting blanket of blue radiance gathered around them and then Precious and Dreamer found themselves transported again to the edge of a dusty dry desert.

"I know we are in a desert but I feel a little like I am still swimming—swimming in the golden lake. No I'm swimming in warped time," said Precious.

There in the middle of a desert, they stood again among scattered, shattered pieces of an ancient fountain. The basin must have stood on a bed of gravel above a water source that dried up, that might have at one time bubbled and spurted a clear stream of water into the air.

Dreamer was staring at the gravel—trying to remember something when an old man with long white hair and a long white beard and a pointed hat, walked up behind him and tapped him on the shoulder.

"Who said that? Did I hear someone say, *warped time*?" The Wizard was looking around.

"Ahaaaa, perhaps it is space that is warped along with time and we are in more than one parallel time-place."

He joined in the chant.

"OMMMMMMmmmmmmmmmmm—"

Precious was wishing for water and imagining a narrow stream of water spurting up into the air. She looked up and then she noticed a black speck in the air—a black bird flying toward them.

The bird was carrying something in its beak. Whatever it was sparkled in the sunlight. Precious pointed at the bird and then looked again at the man who had so suddenly appeared beside them.

"He must be the Wizard."

The black bird flew in a straight line toward them. The Wizard raised his hand and the black bird back-pedaled its wings and flew around and around where the fountain used to stand. The Wizard pointed to his shoulder and finally the bird settled down there.

"What do you carry to us?" the Wizard said to the crow as he took a very small bottle from its beak.

Precious felt a pulsing in her ears and in her feet—a vertical swirling from head to toe.

"There is some kind of energy coming from that bottle," she whispered.

The Wizard handed her the bottle. The marking on the cork of the bottle startled her. It was more than a carving of a sea shell to her. The shell design on the cork was the missing page of a book of her memories of long ago. She heard her grandmother's voice again.

In a bottle sealed with the mark of a sea shell, there is healing magic. One can be well again, can be healed with just a few drops.

Precious remembered her skeptical friends words.

It is just a story. Never was. Never could be such a miraculous healing substance.

Precious was distraught and mumbling.

" I am thirsty and in a desert with Dreamer and a Wizard? A crow carries a bottle. Could it be *the* bottle—the bottle of a magic healing potion?"

There was lightning in the sky and rolling thunder. Clouds were forming above them. It looked like there might be a sudden down pour in the desert.

Precious looked up at two huge clouds. There was a swirling wind. Did it write across clouds? It looked like faint black letters across one cloud spelled U N K N O W I N G. Letters across another cloud spelled K N O W I N G.

Dreamer was pointing up and then staring at the Wizard.

The Wizard looked up at the clouds.

"What could it be that writes on clouds—that names them?"

Precious asked, "Could it be that what is lost is found again and again?"

As Precious spoke cloud shadows passed over the ancient fountain. The shadows seemed to be fleeing from sun beams breaking thru some other clouds.

Precious exclaimed, "Sparkles in mid air."

Dreamer shook his head.

"How can there be reflections, so many reflections floating, rippling, waving in mid-air?"

Precious gasped, "A castle suspended, floating above this desert. What is it? How could it be?"

Just then, there was a commotion, like the pounding of hoofs—like horses on a dead run. A commanding stallion, the white stallion with an ochre spot around one eye, led a whole herd of horses—blacks and whites and many others of mixed and different colors.

They were kicking up dust—galloping, stomping and forming a wide circle beside the ancient dried up fountain.

What had been invisible became visible—a crystal clear pyramidal structure descended around the horses. They continued to stamp their feet in a strange off-beat rhythm inside the structure.

"There they are Talking Horse, Colt and Colt's mother but she looks like a grandmother now," said Dreamer. "And Colt is no longer a colt."

There was an uneasy silence for a few moments.

"No, no," Precious screamed. "How could horses disappear before our very eyes—here one minute and gone the next?"

Dust settled. Dreamer shook his head. There was another awesome silence in the desert. Nothing moved. Dreamer, Precious, The Crow and The Wizard didn't say a word. They all fell into a kind of reverie until the cricket's strumming woke them.

"Well, it's about time. I was beginning to wonder if I might have to tell a story to myself."

And so the cricket began: Once upon a time, a thirsty cricket came to a storytelling place and waited and waited for the listeners to arrive. I knew they were out there somewhere—time-travelers leaving what has been crystallized behind them. They were destined to come together again in the magic of a Oneness from the Many.

The cricket's voice dropped. Dreamer and Precious had to strain to hear its chirps.

What you do in the future can change the past. Our life-giving underground spring revives.

Cricket took a sip of water condensed on the underside of a shattered piece of fountain and paced around muttering.

"The horses have done their part. They have entered the crystal clear pyramid and stamped out the rhythm. They have gone on but something is missing."

"Light baskets, the baskets must be found, must be returned."

The cricket waved its antennae and whispered.

"In the shards of an ancient fountain, how long have I been waiting for you to take me with you?"

A hot desert wind was blowing, stirring up a kind of dry bantering and then its very nature changed as if it sensed the travelers were listening—were hearing what it had to tell them.

The pregnant breeze had its own story to drop on them.

You do not see it but I carry a river. I take it to its appointed destination.

The cricket was silent, listening. The Wizard stroked his beard. Precious spoke to the desert wind.

"The only river I know is far behind us. Dreamer tells me that rivers sometimes rage in a desert and that trying to cross a desert can be dangerous."

"He pointed it out to me—evidence that desert rivers carve canyons and scour dry washes before they grow faint of heart, dry up and disappear."

The wind swirled and whirled and replied.

"Yes, a river can be like that and many fearful rivers rage but there is no reason for a river to dry up. An adventurous river hears my intriguing tales, about faraway places and it allows itself to be transformed, to be lifted up into my arms. I carry it over deadly dry deserts. I carry it to a place where it can begin again—a place it could not reach otherwise."

A mist was forming. Golden drops of water were finding their way into gravel and then into a precious containing chamber below broken fountain parts.

Dreamer looked at Precious.

"I remember taking food and water to Talking Horse. Where did you get those two baskets? Are they light baskets? What happened to them? Could we ever find them again?"

Dreamer and Precious felt a faint trembling underfoot. They were startled into stillness. Their eyes shifted from one another to the empty pyramid.

The vibrations increased. They felt a pulsing in the soles of their feet—a swirling sensation progressing vertically from knees to throat. There was a horizontal swirling in the chest and pulsing in the palms of the hands, in the ends of their fingers.

"The Wizard and the crow— look at them! What do they know? What are they talking about?" whispered Dreamer.

"Come along. A door is opening for us," the Wizard told the black bird on his shoulder. "And I must look into warped time-space."

The Wizard and the bird stepped into the strange vibrating pyramidal structure and disappeared.

Cricket chirped and chirped and scurried toward the pyramid, ahead of Dreamer and Precious. The vibrations had almost stopped but one cheerful chirp inside the pyramid encouraged the vibrations again and the heavens and the earth seemed to respond.

There was a strong vibration under foot and a rumbling over head. A streak of blue lightning leaped from the top of the pyramid.

Precious was staring at the pyramid. She looked into Dreamer's eyes. Dreamer smiled, tilted his head in a beckoning manner and then shifted his eyes toward the pyramid. Her feet and legs were reluctant to go but she nodded her head, yes. Dreamer's arm was around Precious as three more travelers crossed an invisible threshold.

Ripples

It was 2000, A. D., September, late in the afternoon at Lake Shore Drive, Westville, Ohio. Two travelers, Dr. Andrew Prince and his beloved wife, Pearl Lynn, had just returned from a vacation trip to Colorado. Andrew was mowing an overgrown lawn. His wife was carrying one of the two baskets she found so fascinating in a quaint little souvenir shop.

She was weeding a rock garden beside the lake. Scallop edged dry grass reflections, streaks of fall foliage, the gold of near-by aspen doubloons colored the water.

She was light headed, a little dizzy, looking at the ripples in the lake. She dipped the basket she was carrying into the lake to see if it would carry water. Suddenly—somehow, she found herself in the lake in deep water. It was so cool and peaceful. She was drifting down—down—

Something brushed her hand. Her fingers closed around it. She was falling *into gold reflections in the cool water—so peaceful.*

A voice seemed to whisper in her ear, *kick!* The voice insisted louder and louder— kick Kick KICK YOUR LEGS!

Her legs were so heavy—heavy. She was remembering something about gold and the lake. She was so tired and it was so peaceful and cool there.

Dr. Andrew Prince was walking behind the noisy buzzing of his mower in a kind of reverie—remembering the mountains and the trip home from Telluride.

He was lost in his own thoughts. He had one more, maybe two more passes to make with his mower but his legs didn't want to move.

He was suddenly too tired.

Rest for a moment before I go on— just a little more to do.

He thought he heard her voice.

You can finish it in the morning.

Was it Pearl Lynn? He hesitated, took another step, Then he didn't know why, but he stopped and turned the mower off.

Why didn't I finish the last row of mowing? Quiet—

So quiet—

Gold bars floated across the pond.

Streaks of sunshine thru the pines— aspen and maple leaves—So many golden reflections— a golden pond—

"Chhiiiirrrrrrp—chirp, chirp, chir—irp, chir—irp."

A cricket was singing.

Suddenly he missed Pearl Lynn. He felt a sinking in his belly. He called out to her and ran over to where she had been weeding.

"Precious—Pearl Lynn, where are you?"

She kicked her legs. The water rippled. The top of her head was barely visible. She was sinking down again deeper into the water.

"Dear God, no—No!" he cried out.

He jumped into the pond and dragged her to shore. He rolled her on her side.

"Breathe, breathe." he pleaded.

She was gasping. He waited until he was sure she was breathing and then he ran to the house to dial 911.

"Help! help us. She fell into the water," he screamed into the phone.

He ran back to her and gathered her into his lap and rocked her and rocked her.

"Pearl Lynn, my precious one, don't leave me," he crooned to her.

In the ambulance on the way to the hospital, she was gurgling and mumbling.

"Traveled so far— so far to come home again."

"We're just back from our vacation. We were working in the back yard," he said to the ambulance attendant.

"No," she said. "Where is the wizard?"

"Shhhhhhhh, shhhhhhhhhh everything will be all right," he whispered to her.

He reached over and stroked grey hair that had once been golden. Her hand was clenched. She relaxed her grip. A piece of cork fell to the floor.

"The baskets hold water. Our grandchildren—Ryan and Katie and Nicole—"

He Put a finger to her lips and smiled at her.

"At the right time they'll put on the hats we brought them and their own fortunate events will catch up to them."

She nodded and said, "Listen, I can hear it— a cricket singing."

A fountain bubbles up inside. The travelers I will guide.

What was lost is found again. The way opens to another when.

Andrew was wet and shivering. The ambulance attendant put a cover around Andrew's shoulders.

Suddenly Andrew noticed it on the floor beside her , the cork with a sea shell on it. He ran his thumb over it and then put it in her hand again.

"Do you remember?" he asked her.

She reached for Andrew's hand and whispered.

"My two baskets—you don't suppose—"